SECRETS
OF
LILY
GRAVES

by SARAH STROHMEYER

BALZER + BRAY

An Imprint of HarperCollins Publishers

Balzer + Bray is an imprint of HarperCollins Publishers.

The Secrets of Lily Graves
Copyright © 2014 by Sarah Strohmeyer
www.epicreads.com

ISBN 978-0-06-225960-8

Typography by Erin Fitzsimmons
14 15 16 17 18   CG/RRDH   10 9 8 7 6 5 4 3 2 1
❖
First Edition

For Janet Gross Sonnier and her mother, Ann Gross,
for graciously sharing their own experiences
about the womanly craft of burying the dead

ONE

"Hey, Lily. Wait!"

Erin Donohue made her way up the steep hill, her long, coppery hair fluttering in the breeze as she wove through the tombstones. I couldn't imagine what she was doing here in Hillside Cemetery on a bracing Saturday afternoon when everyone else was at the big football game.

She paused by a large marble angel to catch her breath. "What a coincidence, running into you. Then again, I guess this place is your hangout, huh?"

I snapped a twig in half and tossed it into the wheelbarrow. "Something you want, Erin?" I highly doubted she was here to chat. Erin and I hadn't exchanged a civil word maybe ever.

"Just wondered what you were up to. It's so weird to see you doing this kind of work in a full-length black gown. Don't take this wrong, but have you ever considered even trying to act *normal*?"

I ignored the dig and shook the garbage bag filled with dead foliage, rotting green Styrofoam blocks, and broken pots. My mother routinely volunteered my services to the cemetery commission twice a year, spring and fall. Somehow, Erin must have figured this out.

"Doing some winterizing," I said. "Want to help?"

Erin recoiled as if I'd asked her to bury a body. "Ew, no." She rubbed her bare hands and surveyed our surroundings at the far end of the graveyard. "Geez, it's cold up here. Desolate, too. Not a living soul around."

I tied the bag and got a new one. "Yup."

It was late October, almost Halloween, and though it was just after four, the sun was setting. The woods behind us cast dark shadows across the browning grass and the air was turning raw under the gray sky. I had to get going if I wanted to lock the tools in the shed before the caretaker went home.

Erin was not the type to stop by Hillside Cemetery on a whim. She was more the type to document her super busy life in sparkly pink gel ink on her Blessed Virgin Mary wall calendar, every minute packed with wholesome, youthful activities designed to bring her closer to sainthood. Or Villanova. The two in our town being virtually synonymous.

"Matt came by last night," she said breezily.

Matt was Matt Houser, Erin's longtime boyfriend.

"He wanted to talk about us."

I emptied a container of wilted geraniums into a wheelbarrow. I had no idea why Erin thought a routine visit from Matt was something I would find fascinating. "That's nice." *I guess.*

She tagged along as I tended to the next grave, where a wreath of faded plastic roses covered the brass plaque for a World War II veteran. I bent down to get it and she towered over me, blocking the fading light.

"We broke up."

My fingers gripped the small wreath and I stood, careful to appear nonchalant as I folded it in two. "Seriously?" Okay. That *was* a surprise. Matt and Erin were such a thing that they were referred to in one slurred word, *Mattnerin.* "You have a fight?"

"Not exactly." She pulled herself onto a small black tombstone and scowled. "We're taking a break. But I'm sure he'll come back to me. He can never stay away for long."

Why was she telling this to me, of all people? Erin and I had never been particularly close. In fact, we'd been quite the opposite.

"Well, you know how guys are in their senior year," I said, trying to be diplomatic. "Got to spend their final semesters with their bros and all that."

She swung out her leg, blocking my path. "Um, I don't think bros are the problem. It's more like the *hos*." Her lips twisted. "Or, to be more specific, one ho. You."

I sucked in a breath. "Actually, Matt and I . . ."

"Eh, eh, eh." She tick-tocked her finger. "Correction. There is no Matt and you. Never has been. Never will be."

I bit my lip and remained still, staring at her outstretched leg. There were five rows to go and I didn't want to have to come back. But I also didn't want to get into a confrontation.

"Look, Erin, I have to keep moving if I want to get this finished while there's daylight."

I attempted to sneak by, but she slid off the tombstone and blocked my way. "You're not going anywhere until we hash this out."

The caretaker was in the gatehouse watching the game on TV. My phone was locked in my aunt's car on the street. We were almost in the woods and it was beginning to dawn on me that if something happened, no one would hear me scream.

She took a step forward. I took a step back, my heel hitting the base of a headstone. She was so close, I could smell her breath; it possessed an alarming metallic odor.

"Come on, Erin, cut it out." I gave her a slight push, but she wouldn't budge.

"You tried to turn Matt against me."

My pulse had started to race. I was beginning to panic. "Excuse me," I said, shifting to the right.

Erin shifted to her left. "When he realizes you told him a pack of lies, he'll be back."

"And I'm sure you'll be very happy. Now, if you don't mind . . ."

"I'm the only one he'll ever really love."

If I could just get to the gatehouse, I'd be safe. But the gatehouse was all the way at the bottom of the cemetery road. At least I was in Doc Martens, while Erin was in Frye boots with clunky heels. There was a chance.

And then a gust of wind stirred up a curtain of leaves and I went for it, ducking under her and running as fast as I could, leaving my bag of debris behind. The road was in sight when I stupidly slipped on the damp grass and stumbled.

It was all she needed.

Erin clamped onto my forearm and gave it a cruel

twist, taking her hissy fit to a whole new level. I whimpered as she hauled me upright, and I cursed. I did not deserve this kind of abuse. Lots of girls had practically thrown themselves at Matt. I'd merely been his friend. So why was she taking out her rage on me?

"Stop it," I demanded, my arm pulsing in agony.

"Apologize." She cranked it again. "Say you're sorry for spreading lies!"

I couldn't reply, the pain was so intense. All I could do was reach out and bat her away with my other hand, accidentally scratching her cheek.

"You're pathetic!" She twisted again, and I fell hard on the cold ground.

Erin stood over me, that hair of hers whipping wildly in the breeze. She swung her foot for a sharp kick when I grabbed her other ankle and she veered backward, almost catching the sharp edge of a granite tombstone.

The next thing I knew we were rolling in the grass. I was shocked by both of us. I never fought like this. *Never.* And yet, here was Erin doing whatever she could to maximize damage—yanking my black hair, slapping, biting, and finally digging her nails into the delicate flesh of my forearm.

I reared back in pain and horror as blood gushed out in rivulets, running over my wrists onto the browning grass. Only later did I realize that her nails had been filed into seriously badass points.

Leaving me bleeding on the grass, Erin got up and brushed herself off without a second glance.

"You need help," I whispered, hugging my arm.

"Do I? I don't think so. I think you're the one who needs help." She peered at the blood cascading down my wrist and smiled in satisfaction. "You should take care of that. Could get infected."

I held my arm tighter. I felt stunned and dizzy as I wobbled upright. *Do not pass out.*

"Well, see you in school Monday, and remember . . ." She did that tick-tocking thing with her finger again. ". . . it's School Spirit Day, so wear your orange! We already know you've got plenty of black."

With those final words, she proceeded down the snaking cemetery road, adjusting her jacket and smoothing her hair, wiping my blood off her fingers onto her jeans. I watched her walk confidently past the gatehouse and greet the caretaker before stepping into her late-model Mini Cooper. A rev of the engine, a U-ey in the turnaround, and she flew up the hill, passing by with a kiss blown out her window.

I stared for a minute, and then my knees buckled and I collapsed, overtaken by a sudden bout of nausea. Beads of sweat popped out along my hairline and I had to grab on to a headstone for support as I resisted sickening gulps of bile.

Obviously, Matt had said something to Erin about me. But what?

It didn't matter. Erin was right. Those two would never really break up and I bet that come Monday morning they'd be in the hall, entwined in their standard embrace by her lockers, all thoughts of Lily Graves forgotten.

But I would never see Erin again.

At least, not alive.

TWO

The worst of all possible scenarios was waiting for me when I got home.

The best would have been an empty house, but that's a lot to ask when you live in a Gothic funeral home with your aunt and grandmother upstairs and your mother down the hall, as well as several not so lively residents in the basement cooler.

Our house used to be a private mansion owned by a nineteenth-century coal baron before coal went bust in the 1930s, along with the rest of Potsdam. My great-grandfather Harold Graves bought it when prices were rock-bottom during the Great Depression, and according to family legend he became a funeral director just so he could have an excuse for owning a place this impractical.

Since then, it had been divided into sitting rooms and parlors, a chapel, several offices, and two apartments, one for my mother and me on the ground floor, and one for grandmother, Oma, on the top. My aunt Boo had her own digs in the renovated carriage house behind the garage.

Boo moonlighted as our embalmer when she wasn't cutting and styling hair at Sassy Cuts—or getting tattoos. The woman was covered in swirls of ink and intricately stenciled words like *Carrion*, which was imprinted across her hips. I had no doubt that if she'd been around, Boo would have quietly cleaned my wounds, poured me a cup of hot chocolate, and listened without judgment.

Instead, I walked in on Mom and her boyfriend, Perfect Bob.

They were in the kitchen—back from a brisk run, judging from their glistening red cheeks and coordinated spandex—chopping mounds of brightly colored autumn vegetables. Lots of purple beets, orange carrots, and the revered dark, leafy kale.

Mom and Bob were insane about kale. If they weren't stir-frying it or pulverizing it and sneaking the glop into brownies, they were baking kale leaves in the oven and crowing about how the bitter, dried, nasty green flakes were *sooooo* much better than potato chips—a blatant lie.

"Hi, sweetie," Mom chirped as she dumped a handful of red peppers in the wok. "It's late. We were getting worried."

We? I cut my eyes to Bob, who bit into a raw carrot and nodded. Bob was what I suspected every single woman in her forties craved. He was tall and fit, with a distinguished smattering of silver in his closely cropped hair. He ran thirty miles a week, helped with the cooking, fixed dripping faucets, and never forgot to lower the toilet seat. That was what made Bob perfect.

That he was also chief of police made him impossible.

Bob zeroed in on my bloodied arm before I had a chance to cover it. "What happened there?"

"Nothing," I lied, as Mom gasped.

"That's not nothing," she cried, rushing around the center island to inspect the damage. "That looks vicious."

I mumbled something about an accident as Mom dragged me to the sink and turned on the water, squirting Palmolive over my wounds.

"Ow!" I yanked my arm back, but Mom was faster, gripping my wrist and forcing me to endure more.

"You've got to get those cuts clean and Palmolive is just as good as anything," she insisted, using a damp dishcloth to remove the dried blood. "Was it some sort of animal? God, I hope it wasn't rabid. Those shots are awful. Did you see if it had a tag?"

She was firing questions so rapidly, I couldn't answer.

"It didn't have a tag," Bob said coolly. "It was a human."

"What?" Mom flipped off the water, for which I was deeply grateful. She glanced over her shoulder at Bob, then at me with alarm. "Lily, is this true?"

I remained silent. The last thing I needed was Mom making a call to the parents of a classmate, like back in fourth grade when Erin's best friend, Kate Kline, spread rumors that our living room was filled with rotting corpses. With that move, Mom pretty much clinched my status as an outsider.

Bob stepped closer and squinted at the gashes. "That must have been some catfight. Who's the lucky fellow?"

Due to the disgusting sexism of his question, I refused to form a real response.

"You wouldn't understand, Bob," I said, laying another sheet of Bounty on the cuts. "It was random."

"A and B is hardly random."

Assault and battery. Bobspeak.

"Do you want to press charges?" he asked.

I shook my head. *No way.*

"If this incident took place at school, you might have to report it under the new antibullying ordinance."

"It didn't," I said. "It was in the cemetery."

"The cemetery!" Bob arched his eyebrows. "What were you doing there on a Saturday evening?"

This was why I had a problem with cops. God forbid you should be found in a graveyard under the age of twenty-one.

"Sacrificing infants to Satan," I replied. "As one does."

"I volunteered her to do some yard work," Mom said, leaning against the sink and signaling with her pursed lips that I should tone down the sarcasm. "I want the name of the person who did this to you, Lily. And don't tell me it's none of my business. I'm your mother and you've been injured. I have a right to know."

I sighed at my mother's constant overprotectiveness. "Okay, but you have to swear not to immediately get on the phone or go to the principal claiming that I'm a victim of bullying."

"I'll do whatever I want, thank you."

My arm was bleeding through the paper towels. I ripped off another sheet and covered it. "Erin Donohue."

Mom dropped her jaw. "That lovely girl did *this*?"

"She's not so lovely, Mom. I've been trying to tell you that forever. Seriously, she is Lucibitch." I made a mental note to share this incredible new nickname with Sara, my best friend and fellow Erin Donohue victim.

Bob said, "Who?"

"You remember Erin," Mom said. "You gave her a Crime Stoppers Award last spring for turning in those kids who were 'selling' pot."

They were hardly selling. They'd brought a bag to school with about enough marijuana in it to stone a squirrel. Erin had jumped at the chance to rat them out in order to add another accolade to her college résumé.

"Oh, yeah. The skinny redhead. I liked her drive." Bob smiled. He was a big fan of ambition. "Isn't she the one who started that virginity group?"

I rolled my eyes.

"The Purity Pact," Mom said, adding pointedly, "Now, *there's* a good Catholic girl."

As if I should have been ashamed for not leading a clique of hypocritical whack jobs espousing an antiquated, sexist, and quite frankly primitive philosophy that squarely defines women as chattel.

Bob turned to me. "You're not in the Purity Pact, are you?"

"Dude, seriously. Do I seem like the type to join a cult of virgins?"

The tips of his ears turned pink.

Thankfully, this interrogation was cut short by the sudden ringing of our business phone. Mom answered it and retrieved a stack of yellow Post-its and a pen we keep at the ready.

"You want to know how much to *burn a body*?" she repeated for our benefit.

Bob made a face.

"Um," Mom continued, "when did your loved one pass?"

We watched Mom's expression transform from mild annoyance to downright shock.

"So, your grandfather hasn't died yet, but you're in the ICU and the doctors assure you it will be any time now." She scribbled doodles on the Post-it. "You're from out of town and just doing some comparison shopping while you're here."

To Bob's credit, he flipped the caller the bird.

"I see," Mom said, her brown ponytail bobbing with outrage. "Well, then, I suggest you go with Riccoli and Sons. They're a very reputable funeral home that excels in speedy and affordable cremation."

If by "reputable" you mean a 20 percent markup on everything from obituaries to caskets, I thought, admiring my mother's ability to sound so gracious when she was actually applying the screw.

Mom slammed down the phone and fumed. "I know with business slowing I should have taken that, but . . ."

"You have your ethics," Bob said, going over to her. "And that's why I love you, Ruth." He kissed her lightly on the forehead.

Normally, Mom and Bob's PDAs left me mildly nauseous, but I was so grateful the attention had been directed away from Erin and me that I took advantage of the situation to slip away. I figured that as long as I was careful to keep my cuts out of sight, out of mind, the cemetery claw fest would become a nonissue.

But by then, of course, I'd already dug my grave.

THREE

The call that changed everything came the following afternoon while I was crammed into a casket, up to my eyeballs in white eyelet.

It was one of our more expensive models, solid walnut from the pricey Perpetual line. Oma pronounced it a "real beaut," with intricate inlay and artistic detailing, all of which was about to be completely undone by a mouse that my grandmother claimed to have seen hiding in one of its padded corners.

"Lure it out with cheese," Boo urged, slipping a slim piece of cheddar into my outstretched hand, "and I'll put a bag over it and take it outside."

Boo was a softie when it came to both the dead and

the living and rarely left a movie without dabbing her eyes and blowing her nose, even comedies with sappy romantic endings. Upon seeing my cuts, for example, she'd wrapped me in a bear hug and murmured, "Tell me who did this, sweetie, and I'll get a guy I know to break both his legs."

It was strangely comforting, in a mildly violent way.

Oma found an empty urn and held it over her head. "Well, I for one am not about to stand around waiting for it to crawl up my dress," she announced. "I'm going on the offensive." At that very moment, the tiny critter reemerged and scrambled over the toes of her new Anne Klein shoes. Oma didn't even notice.

"There it is!" Mom shrieked, hopping onto a stool and pointing hysterically.

The mouse went for it, dashing across the carpet toward the sanctuary of the curtains.

"Die! Die! Die!" My tiny grandmother, who was in her seventies and about the size and height of an Oompa Loompa, brought the silver urn down from over her head and tried to smash the mouse. Boo stepped in for the block, the urn bouncing on the carpet and missing the rodent by a mousy gray hair.

"That was cruel," Boo said. "It has a right to live, just like everything else."

"Eeep! There it is again!" Mom screeched as

the creature scuttled out from under our prize blue Potomac coffin, the one no one ever bought because it cost more than $5,000.

The funeral home phone rang. Mom gingerly stepped off the stool and ran on her tiptoes to her office to get it.

Oma retrieved the urn and chucked it bowling ball–style. I could have sworn the mouse was a goner.

"No!" Boo gasped, rushing to scoot the terrified little thing into a paper bag. She finally caught it and went outside to let it free in the garden, while I got out of the casket so Oma could inspect it for mouse poop.

"Normalcy," she said, "is far too underrated by you people."

I didn't know if by "you people" she meant teenagers, or Boo and me. I suspected the latter.

Something made us stop, and we both turned to see Mom, her lips set in a firm line, clutching the phone.

"Pickup at the Donohues'," she said flatly.

Oma covered her mouth. "The father?"

Mom shook her head slightly. "The girl who's in Lily's class." And then, with a look I'd never seen before, one with so much pain it almost made me afraid, Mom whispered, "I'm sorry, Lily. It's Erin."

"Huh?" I said, my muddled brain assuming Erin was the one who'd called it in.

"About an hour ago," Mom said, "her parents came home and found her dead upstairs."

My peripheral vision went black as though I'd stepped into a tunnel. Time slowed. My ears rang. Nothing made sense.

"Not Erin," I said, feeling confused. Surely, she meant some other Donohue. A different Erin. Obviously, Mom had gotten it wrong.

"I'm so, so sorry," Mom said again. "This is absolutely horrible."

The floor swayed and I teetered. Thinking quickly, my mother scooped me up with one arm and kept me steady. My breathing was heavy and I realized I was disassociating. It was as if my soul had left my body and was now watching from above, totally detached.

I've heard that when you die you see your life replayed like a movie. In this case, I saw Erin's, starting with when she'd appeared in the cemetery Saturday and going backward. There she was climbing the steps of our high school's stage to receive yet another award junior year. At the junior prom being crowned queen by Matt. Introducing an assembly about the dangers of underage drinking. Leading a prayer group after the school shootings in Virginia. Delivering a vicious spike in volleyball. Whispering behind her hands when Sara and I passed by her in the middle school cafeteria. Slipping a nasty anonymous Valentine into my decorated shoebox in fourth grade. Pushing me off the swing in second grade.

Erin Donohue had been a thorn in my side for thirteen years. That she was gone was simply impossible. It had to be a mistake.

"Accident?" Oma asked.

"Nooo," Mom said carefully. "Appears to have been a suicide."

Suicide.

A wave of guilt hit me broadside. Erin had taken her own life because she'd gotten it into her head that Matt had dumped her for me. It was crazy, because Erin had everything—looks, smarts, drive, friends, even money—but you never knew, did you? More often than not it was the little things that brought you down.

Oh God, I was going crazy myself.

"Lily?" Oma asked. "Are you okay?"

"I think she's hyperventilating," Mom said. "We need to . . ."

My knees gave out then. My mother's arm kept me upright, and for once I appreciated her rock-solid stability. "This is all my fault," I said. "She killed herself because of me."

"Nonsense," Oma commanded. I tried to focus, but

my grandmother came in blurry. "Clearly, the child was plagued with demons. First she attacks you, then she takes her own life. If there's anything to blame, it's some underlying mental illness."

"Oma is right," Mom said, lifting my chin with her slim finger. "This is a devastating tragedy, and it's only natural to want to point the finger, even at yourself, but please don't go there. That doesn't help anyone."

Their words, while well-intentioned, began to lose their meaning. Whatever Mom and Oma were saying didn't matter. At the core was the truth. That's what I needed to discover.

The truth.

"Lily?"

Mom was peering at me earnestly. Oma was nowhere to be found, and I was on the pastel floral couch in our front office. I didn't even remember how I got there.

She handed me a glass of water, which seemed like such a cliché.

"I'm not thirsty," I said, pushing it away.

"Yes, you are. Drink it. Just a sip."

I did so to indulge her, and suddenly I couldn't get enough. I was as dry as a desert inside. Three glasses of water later, I was sitting up and beginning to gather my wits.

Erin Donohue was dead. She'd killed herself.

I needed Sara. Stat.

"I know this is difficult," Mom said, "but if you're okay by yourself, I wonder if you could answer the phones while Boo and I retrieve Erin's body. Oma has gone over to the Donohues' ahead of us to help them fill out paperwork."

"Absolutely," I said, trying to rise to the occasion. This was a huge client for our business, and already I'd caused a delay by fainting in the casket room and keeping Mom from doing her job.

"Will you be all right?" she asked.

"Sure. I'm sorry. I don't know what came over me."

"Only the worst thing possible. Don't expect to recover from this anytime soon."

Mom knew from experience how bad this was, having dealt with death on a personal as well as professional level for eons.

"By the way," she added, "it's probably best if we keep this quiet for now. It won't help the Donohues if our funeral home becomes gossip central, which it will be if Sara hears about this, especially since Erin interned for her father last summer." She gave me one last knowing look and left.

I waited two whole minutes before I got out my phone and called my best friend.

"It doesn't seem real," Sara said, sounding close to tears. "Okay, so Erin and I were never what you'd call buddy-buddy, but this? This is the worst thing ever!"

I mumbled in begrudging agreement.

"Erin was in our living room just the other day, sitting on the kitchen stool talking to Mom and Dad, reminiscing about all the silly mistakes she'd made when she started interning."

"Did anything seem off?" I asked.

"Aside from her hypercheerfulness? No. But by then she'd already decided to do herself in. They say that's the way it is with suicides."

Erin's family lived around the corner from Sara in the same cookie-cutter development of oversize houses with humongous garages and kitchens built for hosting small conventions. Because their families were so friendly, Sara's dad, Dr. Ken, had offered Erin an unpaid job in his pediatric practice at the hospital, babysitting kids in the waiting room while the parents were in appointments with their other children.

The idea had been Erin's, since she was thinking of majoring in pre-med at Villanova and also, again, because of that college résumé she was forever building.

All that hard work, all those great grades and spectacular extracurriculars . . . for slit wrists in a bathtub?

None of this felt right.

"She wasn't that hypercheerful when I saw her Saturday afternoon," I said. "She went berserk and attacked me for no reason."

"Well, like you said yourself, Lil, she probably got the wrong idea about you and Matt."

Sara had never been a big fan of Matt Houser because he was one of those cute jocks with, as she put it, "a third bicep for a brain." However, I'd always suspected there was more to it than that. Sara resented Matt because ever since he'd asked me to tutor him in US History last summer, she and I hadn't hung out as much. On Tuesday and Thursday evenings, when I normally would have been over at her house lounging by her family's sweet inground pool, Matt and I had been in the (air-conditioned) public library downtown or in the cool shade of the cemetery studying. It was definitely a wedge in our friendship.

"My relationship with Matt is purely platonic," I said, repeating what I'd told her a zillion times before.

"I've got news for you. Members of the opposite sex who call each other every night before they go to sleep while they're in bed are more than just friends."

I felt myself go hot. "It's nothing—he just razzes me

about being such a morbid nerd."

"His teasing is adorable and you know it. And so did Erin. Not that you should blame yourself for her suicide," Sara was quick to add. "I'm just stating facts."

Sometimes Sara's love of "facts" got on my nerves, but then I'd remember that she couldn't help herself, because her whole goal in life was to become a famous criminal prosecutor. The only television she watched was back-to-back true-crime shows on Investigation Discovery about deadly women and Southern murderers and serial killers—necessary preparation, she claimed, for Harvard Law.

"Okay," I said, "but those 'facts' are wrong."

"Possibly," she conceded. "But Matt *did* come to you first about whether he and Erin should split. So even if you didn't want to be roped into their drama, you were."

I would never forget that night, how Matt scaled the wall of our garden and tapped on my bedroom window, scaring me out of my wits. I'd climbed out and both of us stood there in the warm September air, what we didn't say more important than what we did. He shoved his hands in his pockets and leaned close. I had stayed still. As much as my body was dying to kiss him, I refused to be "that" girl.

A no-win situation.

"I never told him to break up with Erin," I said. "I

remained totally neutral, the same way I was toward you when you were breaking up with Ty."

"If I recall, your exact words were 'Dump that idiot, Sara, before he dumps you.'"

"I was right, wasn't I?"

"Yup. But a monkey could have called that." She paused. "How's Matt dealing, anyway?"

I checked my phone to see if any messages had come in while we'd been talking. "I don't know. He hasn't replied to any of my texts."

"When did you last hear from him?"

"Friday, when he wrote that on a scale of one to ten in movies, one being anything with subtitles and ten being any movie with Seth Rogen, *Ted* was a twenty." That seemed so long ago.

"I thought you told him about Erin's attack."

"I did. I even sent him a photo of my cuts and wrote, 'You won't believe what happened.' You'd think that'd be intriguing enough for him to text right back, but I guess not."

Sara went silent for a bit. "And you never heard from him again?"

"No."

"Fascinating."

I didn't like the way Sara said that, as if she were concluding a cross-examination before a rapt jury.

"What are you thinking?" I asked.

"You don't want to know."

But I knew.

I think a part of me always had.

That night, after Mom and Boo had come home and gone to bed, I tiptoed upstairs to Mom's office to conduct a search. Since the cardinal sin of morticians was gossip, Mom wouldn't be forthcoming with info now that she had a professional obligation to keep her client's confidentiality. So if I wanted to learn anything about Erin's suicide, I would have to break a few rules.

Fortunately, rule-breaking was one of my better-honed skills.

Erin's file was the top entry in Mom's Word documents and thoroughly disappointing in its ordinariness. There would be calling hours on Thursday at the funeral home, followed by a funeral on Saturday at St. Anne's. The Donohues had filled in the standard form Oma used to assemble an obituary for the local paper. It listed Erin's awards and achievements, survivors, and places to submit donations (ASPCA) instead of flowers. Of course, people would send them anyway.

I closed out, logged off, and was pushing back Mom's chair when I spied the thin white sheets of paper curling out of the fax machine. I turned them over and smoothed them flat. The letterhead of the Potsdam Police Department was stamped on top.

> *TO: Robert R. Amidon, Chief of Police*
> *FROM: Detective Joe Henderson*
> *RE: REQUEST FOR THE PENNSYLVANIA*
> *STATE POLICE CRIME LAB*
> *DEPARTMENT USE ONLY—*
> *CONFIDENTIAL*

It appeared to be an internal police memo. It was so unlike Perfect Bob to release something this top secret, much less fax it to Mom. Had to be bad.

> *At approximately 1420 hours on Sunday, October 28, Potsdam Police Department dispatch received a 911 call from a female identifying herself as Elaine Donohue, reporting a nonresponsive female, age 17, in the upstairs bathroom of their house at 322 Maple Drive. Ambulance and rescue personnel were sent to the scene, along with Officer Crowley and myself.*
>
> *Upon arrival, I observed the body of a teenage girl lying face up in a bathtub, several lacerations on both wrists, naked aside from a pink towel. Both the edges of the towel and the water in the bath appeared to be red with blood. Emergency personnel confirmed*

that the female was indeed deceased. The medical examiner was immediately notified and the area secured at 1448 hours.

Preliminary observations revealed that on the tile floor by the bathtub was an ordinary 8 oz. drinking glass containing clear fluid, which I marked for analysis. There was no obvious evidence of razors, knives, or other sharp objects that might have been used to inflict the lacerations. Nor could any blood be superficially observed outside of the immediate bathtub vicinity.

Riley and Elaine Donohue, owners of the house, identified the female as their daughter, Erin Anne Donohue, age 17. Riley Donohue advised that he and his wife had returned to their home at approximately 1400 hours after spending the weekend closing up their summer cabin in the Poconos. Their daughter had remained at home, as she frequently had done in the past.

Mr. Donohue advised that the screen door to the back patio was open and the other doors locked when he and his wife returned. Erin's car, a 2012 Mini Cooper, was in the garage. The family dog, Sparkle, had defecated on the living room rug, indicating it had not been let outside that morning.

Mrs. Donohue went upstairs and located her

daughter in the master bath. She called for her husband, a former volunteer firefighter, who attempted first aid, including a heart massage and mouth-to-mouth resuscitation, while Mrs. Donohue called 911. Officer Crowley and I arrived five minutes later, along with the Center Valley Regional Rescue.

At 1530 hours, I interviewed the Donohues' next-door neighbors, Eugene and Joan Krezky of 320 Maple Drive. They advised that at approximately 2200 on October 27, they telephoned the Donohues to complain of loud music from what appeared to be a party. Several minutes later, three females exited the premises and left in a "Jeep-like" vehicle. The music stopped.

At 2230, Mrs. Krezky accompanied their dog into the backyard before going to bed. From her vantage point, she was able to see into the Donohues' living room window, where she observed a female she identified as Erin Donohue arguing loudly with an unidentified male approximately six feet in height.

Based on the above observations, along with the facts that, after a thorough search, no sharp objects were located near the deceased victim, and that the only blood found at the scene was in the bathtub, it is my belief that Erin Anne Donohue was the victim of a homicide.

Considering the sensitive nature of the case, the age of the victim, the residential location of the crime, and the potential for DNA as well as other highly technical laboratory analysis of evidence to identify the perpetrator(s), I am officially requesting the assistance and use of the Pennsylvania State Police Crime Lab as well as supporting personnel.

Respectfully submitted on Oct. 28 at 2020 hours,

Detective Joseph L. Henderson.

The paper fell from my hand and fluttered to the floor while I sat there, stunned.

Homicide.

Erin hadn't taken her own life. Someone else had. The idea that a stranger or, worse, a person Erin knew—possibly a person *I* knew—had invaded her house, slit her wrists, and then left without a trace, was so terrifying that I went ice-cold.

Especially after I read the neat block letters in Perfect Bob's handwriting at the bottom of the page.

KEEP LILY AWAY FROM MATT HOUSER

FOUR

You'd think that, the day after Erin was found dead in her bathtub, there would be grief counselors to greet us at the school door. When T.J. Hawkes ran his snowmobile into a tree last winter, you couldn't take a step without some patchouli-scented earth mother rushing to offer herbal tea and tented fingers. But come Monday morning, there was no administrator in the lobby aside from the nurse, who was always there to nag the ADD students into taking their Adderall.

The single official acknowledgment of Erin's passing was during homeroom, when Principal Kemple got on the intercom to request a moment of silence in honor of the senior class president. He didn't even use the D-word, supposedly because Kemple was cautioned against "canonizing" Erin for fear of copycats. As if we'd have killed ourselves to be mentioned in the morning announcements.

I don't know why I didn't tell Sara about the classified police memo—maybe because despite my differences with Perfect Bob, I didn't want to get him in trouble for leaking it to Mom.

Or maybe I was trying to protect Matt, because Sara would have immediately invented a bazillion theories for why he'd murdered Erin, along with motives, methods, and evidence. If I'd told her about Bob's note, Sara would have done everything in her power to keep me from having any contact with Matt. It would have been 24/7 of her saying "I told you so."

"Where are the Tragically Normals?" I asked her at lunch.

The head table, usually reserved for Erin, Matt, his best pal, Jackson (too cool for a first name), and Erin's ladies-in-waiting—Kate Kline, Allie Woo, and Cheyenne Day—was ominously deserted, the chipped fake wood laminate sparkling under the fluorescent cafeteria lights.

"At home trying to deal, probably," Sara said, stirring her yogurt. "Can you imagine? Never in a million years did they expect that one of them would kill herself. Then again, those types never do."

Of course. That's why we'd dubbed them the Tragically Normals, because they were truly living the ultimate high school experience. Good grades? Check. Lettering in sports? Check. Nice cars, cute boyfriends, adorable girlfriends, clear skin, ideal physical proportions? Check, check, check, check, and check.

Sara and I, on the other hand, were kind of the Happily Twisted. I'd been warped, for better or worse, growing up in a funeral home and being lulled to sleep as a toddler by the whirr of Boo's embalming machine injecting pink-tinted formaldehyde into the veins of corpses in the room below. That alone had made me such a freak in elementary school that no one would come to my birthday parties despite my carefully handwritten invitations, pony rides in our huge walled garden, and Oma's spectacular three-tier chocolate cakes.

In fact, the only person who ever dared to sleep over was Sara. She didn't mind the creaky floors of our ancient mansion or the fact that our basement refrigerator contained not ice-cold Cokes, but cadavers on ice. Then again, I suppose Sara had ghosts of her own.

She didn't like to talk about it much, how her birth mother had been so repulsed by Sara's withered left arm that she'd abandoned her at the Russian hospital when Sara was only three days old. It was Sara's mom, Carol, who told me that when she and Dr. Ken arrived at the orphanage in the Khabarovsk region, Sara had been confined to an iron crib for two years, totally neglected. No one had held or played with her, sung her songs, or read her stories. Ever. For six months, Sara screamed whenever Carol tried to pick her up.

Of course, you'd never know that now. Carol and Ken dote on her every whim, and Sara's such a willowy white blonde with crystal blue eyes that boys swoon. She's also become an expert at concealing her arm, so that by the time a guy falls madly in love, she could be half lizard and he wouldn't care.

Perhaps that explained why, even as far back as second grade, Erin started picking on her, not because of what Sara was, but because of what she would someday become: Erin's biggest competition.

I drove by Matt's house on my way home from school that day. Big mistake.

Usually, Sara did the driving, but she was in Philly meeting with the pricey college counselor her parents had hired to get her into an Ivy League school. With the early decision application to Yale due Thursday, this was the final edit before she sent in the whole package—2400 SATs, a 3.9 GPA transcript, and an essay about being a Russian orphan. So there was no room in her busy schedule for stalking.

That's what Sara would have called my drive across town to Westwood, where Matt lived in a simple brick house with his mother and dad, an assistant football coach at Potsdam High. I was just checking to make sure he wasn't too lonely or guilt-ridden. Good Samaritan, totally platonic friend—that was me!

The entire football team, along with a posse of Tragically Normals, was gathered in Matt's front yard, hugging and crying. Kate and Cheyenne stood side by side with raccoon eyes, mascara streaming down their cheeks. Allie sat on the grass, face in her hands.

But there was no sign of Matt.

"Yo, freak!"

A body hit the front end of my car and suddenly Matt's best friend, Jackson, was on the hood. I slammed the brakes and swallowed my guts.

He rolled off, totally fine, and sauntered over to my window. "What's up?" he asked.

I'd never particularly liked Jackson. There was something about his smarmy grin and the cocky, yet insecure way he always had to draw attention to himself that was mildly disgusting. It was as if he expected every girl to throw herself at his feet just because he had sandy blond surfer hair and was our soccer team's best attacker.

"Driving home from school," I said, embarrassed

to have been caught spying.

Jackson grinned. "Kind of out of your way, isn't it?"

I gripped the steering wheel. In my peripheral vision, I could see that Kate, Allie, and Cheyenne had gathered in a clump of perfection and were peering at us curiously.

"Gotta go," I said, shifting into drive.

"If you're looking for him, forget it," Jackson said. "Word is, he's on house arrest. Not allowed to see anyone . . . even you, freak."

"I wasn't looking—"

"Don't start. We know that's why you're here." He stepped back, but still held on to my car door. "I'd ask you to join us, but turns out no one wants you around, Lily Graves. You're like the Grim Reaper, man, giving everyone the creeps with your witchy wardrobe." He held up his hands and wiggled his fingers.

The trio of TNs stifled their laughter.

I stepped slowly on the gas and, after a fleeting fantasy of driving over Jackson's feet, headed down the street. In my rearview, I could see Kate, Allie, and Cheyenne burst into hysterics.

Three girls were spotted coming out of Erin's house on Saturday night, according to the police report.

Kate. Allie. Cheyenne.

FIVE

It was after five when Mom and her assistant, Manny, returned from the autopsy with Erin in the back of our hearse. It beeped slowly down the incline in reverse and stopped. Mom emerged, looking frazzled, while Manny proceeded to the rear, flipped open the latch, and removed the gurney.

My gaze fell to the black vinyl body bag. That was all that was left of Erin. Bones and rotting flesh. Mom and I stood side by side quietly while Manny rolled the gurney through the garage door and into our peach-colored prep room, where that night Boo would perform her magic. With my assistance.

"Do you have a moment?" Mom asked, gingerly

pulling off her leather gloves finger by finger. "I'd like to have a talk."

This was more of a command than a request.

We headed upstairs and down the blue-carpeted hall, with its creamy walls and framed paintings of pastoral landscapes, along with a zillion boxes of tissues. Though our rooms were designed to induce calm, I was feeling anything but.

She ushered me into her office, the pretend one for meeting with clients, not the real one upstairs loaded with files and her computer. This room was all tidy tranquillity. The air was scented with lavender and a small machine emitted white noise to mask the sound of weeping clients. Two green leather chairs faced a mahogany desk, above which hung a framed photo of five-year-old me, smiling gap-toothed between Aunt Boo and a young version of my mother, our hands positioned protectively on the shoulders of Oma.

Mom took her usual position behind the desk. "We have a problem."

"I gathered as much," I said, perching on the chair across from her.

"Bob would like you to come down to the station and undergo a buccal smear."

She could not be serious. A buccal smear was where they swabbed the inside of your cheek to get a sample of your DNA. You didn't have to watch as many true-crime shows as Sara did to know that much.

"I'm not happy about it," Mom continued. "Needless to say, Bob and I have differing opinions, but he has finally managed to convince me that this is for your own good, and he's promised that this will be the end of your involvement in Erin's case."

I said, "Case? What case? Erin committed suicide, end of story, right?" Since Mom had no idea that I'd snooped in her upstairs office, I had to play dumb.

She exhaled through her teeth. "Not exactly. Now, I know this is upsetting, but it seems there is evidence that Erin was, well, I guess the only right word is . . . *murdered.*"

I popped my eyes wide in feigned disbelief. "No way! That's awful!"

Mom did a calming-motion thing with her hands. "Try not to panic, Lily. You're perfectly safe. Bob says the police have a suspect on their radar, and they won't let him out of their sight until he's arrested."

This was why I was panicked. I perked up. "Tell me it's not someone from school."

"I can't say who it is, but you'll just have to trust me for now that everything's under control."

"Then why do the police need to do that swab thingy if they already have a suspect?"

Mom began tidying the desk, rearranging the stapler and magnetic paper clip holder with her usual OCD efficiency, a sure sign that this was driving her crazy. "The way Bob explained it was that if Erin fought off her attacker then his DNA might be under her nails, and they needed to separate it from yours."

"Oh." I deconstructed what Mom said, looking for clues. "So they think it was definitely a guy who did it."

My mother shrugged. "Supposedly, a neighbor saw Erin in an argument with a boy on Saturday night and . . . How come you're not more surprised? I thought for sure you'd be shocked that Erin didn't commit suicide."

"I am. I am!" I brought my hand to my chest to emphasize my ignorance. "It just hasn't sunk in yet."

Mom knit her brows, reflecting on this explanation. "At any rate, it would be best if you didn't announce this to the world, including Sara. And definitely not to Matt Houser."

"I get Sara, but why not Matt?"

"I have no idea," she said, her elbow accidentally bumping the stapler to the floor. "Anyway, the best thing for you to do is to let the police handle it, sweetie." She leaned over to pick up the stapler and resurfaced with the complexion of a tomato. "Let it go."

How could I let go of something so nightmarish as

a nice guy being framed for a murder he didn't commit? "But—"

"No buts," Mom said firmly. "Stay out of it and that's that."

We stared at each other across her desk, and not for the first time I wondered what had happened to this woman.

When I was little, Mom was my own personal goddess. I would imitate her every move, the way she graciously listened and never interrupted our overwrought clients, the discreet manner in which she averted her gaze when grieving families erupted into tears or arguments, often simultaneously. Everyone called me Mini Ruth.

That was fine as long as I played by her rules. But in middle school, when I started dressing the way I wanted, in sweeping black lace and dyed hair to match, Mom got all agitated. She became even more uptight when she found under my bed *The Tibetan Book of the Dead*, along with several mortuary catalogs, dog-eared to beautiful urns and caskets I particularly admired.

"This is not normal," she'd murmur, tracing the lines on my neck where I'd outlined the crucial embalming veins in red Sharpie.

I found that kind of ironic, since I clearly remembered her doing the same to her own body when she was in community college studying for the mortuary science degree she needed to run the funeral home after my father died.

Besides, I figured she'd have been thrilled that her daughter wanted to go into the family business, right? At age eleven, I lusted over custom-built, hand-crafted pine caskets from Vermont the way other girls craved Vera Bradley backpacks. At fifteen, I solo-prepped my first body from head to toe, and the corpse looked so alive Boo proclaimed me a "gifted natural."

Instead, Mom thought I was, as she put it, "acting out."

"Let me see those scratches again," she said with a tilt of her chin.

Reluctantly, I showed her my arm. A healthy dose of Neosporin had reduced the menacing red streaks to faint pink swirls. Even so, my arm was swollen, ugly, and bruised a greenish purple.

She winced. "Is it still painful?"

"You have no idea." I pulled down my sleeves and tried to ignore the burning pain from even that light friction.

"Speaking of Matt, have you heard from him lately?" Mom asked.

This was turning out to be the million-dollar question. I shook my head.

"Can't say I'm disappointed. Matt is a boy with"—
she bit her lower lip—"bad intentions, I think. The
more distance between you two, the better."

But I would never distance myself from Matt. And
Mom knew it.

You could tell by the fear in her eyes.

While my mother supervised a wake, I ate a quick dinner of chicken soup and PB and J at the kitchen table,
accidentally dotting my calculus homework with
sticky purple spots of jam that I tried in vain to erase.
Then I washed the dishes and waited for everyone to
file out into the crisp October air, chatting amicably as
they stepped into their cars and sped off.

It was my job to clear away the coffee cups and cake
crumbs afterward, to refresh the tissue boxes and wipe
the bathroom sinks and run the carpet sweeper everywhere, from the Serenity to the Eternity parlors, with
a stop in between to dust Paradise. Only when those
duties were finished was I free to escape to the prep
room.

"Hey, Lil!" Boo said, turning off her radio. "Perfect
timing. I was just about to come upstairs and get you."

Boo had come straight from working in the hair
salon, so she was still in her professional clothes: a red
faux-leather miniskirt, black fishnet stockings, and

fabulous studded suede boots. Her blond hair had been tinted purple at the ends to match the amethyst stud in her nose. It kind of clashed with the red, but I liked that, and the *K* in *Karma* that peeked out from the cleavage of her white blouse.

"I did what I could. It wasn't easy." Boo waved to Erin, stretched out on the steel table, her autopsy incisions neatly sewed. She was so thoroughly preserved in formaldehyde that her corpse emitted the slightly vinegary smell reminiscent of those fetal pig dissections we did in bio. It burned the insides of my nostrils.

It was odd to see Erin this plasticized and defenseless, her newly washed red hair in a halo around her vacant face, her mouth glued into a pleasant smile. On closer examination, I noticed her inner thighs were riddled with scars, as were her waist and breasts.

Weird.

Boo pointed to Erin's left hand, which was permanently positioned over her right now that the embalming fluid had hardened them in place. "As you can see, she's in need of a manicure. I thought it only fitting that you do the honors."

The crimson polish was chipped and the police had cut all her pointed nails to nubs. My arm throbbed in memory.

"Think you can handle this?" Boo asked gently.

"Sure," I said, getting out the blow-dryer. "Do you want to do hair or makeup?"

Boo chose makeup—Mary Kay cosmetics, since she couldn't stand the morticians' gunk—while I did Erin's hair, blowing it dry, setting it, and brushing out the copper curls. We worked silently in unison, performing an ancient ritual that Graveses have done for generations.

When everything was sprayed into place, I brought out the polish remover, wiped off the crimson, and filed what was left of her ragged nails into blunt harmlessness. Then I painted them an insipid pink.

Boo massaged almond-scented lotion over Erin's skin to keep it dewy-soft. We tacked on underwear and a bra before slicing open the back and arms of a delicate white cashmere turtleneck sweater the Donohues brought to cover their daughter's body. Then we did the same to the black skirt, pinning it to her preserved flesh so it stayed secure. Boo unclasped a string of pearls—apparently a sixteenth-birthday gift—and gently draped them around Erin's neck. A matching pair of studs went next, and finally she was finished.

Erin looked as if she were simply taking a nap when we closed her casket and rolled her away for storage until the viewing on Thursday.

Matt never could understand why I found prepping bodies so satisfying. I wished he were there now, to see.

"How you holding up?" Boo asked as we sanitized the prep room, sterilizing the instruments and scrubbing down all the surfaces with disinfectant. "Your mom says the cops want a DNA test. You okay with that?"

"Do I have a choice?" I spritzed bleach over the steel table. Cleanup: my least favorite duty.

"Probably not." Boo peeled off her latex gloves, stepped on the garbage can pedal to open the lid, and tossed them in. "For what it's worth, Oma and I are both of the opinion that you should have a lawyer present."

I stopped washing, incredulous that my aunt and grandmother thought it was this serious. "Don't tell me you two think *I* murdered Erin."

"*Puh-leeze.* But you know this is Potsdam RFD, and the cops here have the IQ of doughnuts." Boo rested her elbows on the table, right where I'd disinfected. "The thing is, your mom has to stay in the good graces of the police in order to keep getting the transport referrals."

"And a date for New Year's Eve."

Boo diplomatically ignored my reference to Perfect

Bob. "All I can say is that if your dad were alive, he'd insist on legal representation for you. Period."

Boo was my father's baby sister, so named because she'd been a "boo-boo" baby, born when Oma was forty-seven and, as Oma herself often said, "frankly, just too tired to give a damn." In fact, at age thirty, my aunt was closer to me than to Mom—in more ways than one.

"Thanks, Auntie."

She tapped my nose with her finger. "Just try to hang in there, Lily. This too shall pass."

Before I went to bed, I went from door to door, window to window, locking each one in our ground-floor apartment, which was attached to the funeral home section of our mansion. There was only one window I couldn't completely secure. It was the one in my room, facing the garden, the one Matt had tapped the night he asked me if he should break up with Erin.

That was the window I watched until I was eventually overcome by sleep.

SIX

Matt did visit me that night, in a way.

I dreamed it was last summer and he and I were hanging out in the cemetery. There was brilliant sunshine all around us and I was so incredibly happy that Erin was alive, I didn't want to wake up. I wanted to stay in the past when my only worries were whether I was destined to graduate from high school unkissed—or if Matt would break the curse.

Matt had been an enigma to me before he called me out of the blue last July, totally panicked. Being the assistant football coach, his father had delivered an ultimatum: retake the US History final from junior year and pass, or spend the last semester of high school football on the bench.

His parents wouldn't let Erin tutor him because she was his girlfriend and they thought he wouldn't get any work done with her across the table. I, on the other hand, wasn't even a friend, and since I'd aced the class and was the class freak to boot, the Housers considered me an ideal choice. Safe. Sexless. Smart.

He offered to pay me twenty bucks a session and I figured, What the heck? Easy money. Besides, I had nothing better to do than organize Boo's supply cabinet and clean the parlors. So I said yes.

To my mind, Matt was one of those dumb jocks who had just enough brains to take advantage of his hotness. He was tall and built, with a carefree way of strutting that conveyed a sense of superiority. In the off-season, he let his brown hair grow long, falling right below his jawline. Sometimes it appeared stringy, although that might have been more from his attempt to achieve a certain look rather than poor hygiene, because otherwise he was fairly put together.

His style ran to Chucks that were hardly smudged and bright white T-shirts under a meticulously maintained orange-and-black Potsdam Panthers letter jacket with his chosen number—7—in homage to legendary Pittsburgh Steelers QB Ben Roethlisberger.

Matt had rarely bothered to acknowledge my

presence, except when I came to honors history in full Morticia Addams regalia, and then he'd give me a long, lingering stare while Erin prudishly pursed her lips and sniggered.

How he'd gotten into honors history was a mystery in itself, though that might have explained the failing grade. He usually slouched in the back with one leg extended, half-asleep, while next to him Erin with her array of pens (color-coded for cross-reference) sat up straight, prefacing her comments with "I just feel" or "In my opinion."

He rarely spoke unless the brownnosers were trying to score points, in which case he'd exclaim in a bad British accent, "Excellent argument, sir!" or "Yes, yes. Well stated. Touché!" This was usually followed by hearty applause and suppressed laughter from the rest of us.

But there was one incident that always made me wonder if there was more to Matt than his *Friday Night Lights* exterior. It happened sophomore year when Sara and I were innocently eating our lunch in the Potsdam High cafeteria along with our mutual friend Tam.

Tam was not a small person. All her life she'd struggled with her weight. But she was supersmart and really sweet. I'd never heard her say a mean thing about anyone, ever. Which was why it was so incredibly jerklike of Jackson to snatch up Tam's Diet Coke that day and make fun of her for drinking it to offset the calories of a coconut-and-chocolate Magic Bar.

"Oh, yeah, like this is going to help," he scoffed, holding up the soda for everyone to see. "Forget it, girl. You'll always be an F.U.B."

Fat. Ugly. Bitch.

Tam just froze, the Magic Bar halfway to her mouth. It was so over-the-top that I was tempted to let him have it myself, when in stepped Matt.

"Dude, like you're one to talk." He yanked up Jackson's shirt to reveal a surprisingly flaccid gut and gave it a loud slap.

Everyone laughed. Even Tam smiled as Jackson pulled down his shirt and told Matt where to shove it.

Matt patted her shoulder. "Ignore my friend. He's just jealous because his mommy didn't put a cookie in his lunch today."

Jackson socked him in the arm.

"Ouch?" Matt said, questioningly. "Was that supposed to hurt? Because I didn't even feel it."

"Not sure if you can handle a real one," Jackson said, pretending to make a fist.

I eyed Kemple, who was craning his neck to see what was going on. "Watch it, guys. You're about to get busted."

"Graves!" Matt shouted, as if just noticing my presence. "How nice to see you out of the coffin. Is it a full moon? Or were you in need of fresh blood?"

"Actually, I was running a little low on stupid. But you two took care of that."

Matt hesitated a beat, gave me a curious look, and then broke into a grin. "Glad we could accommodate." He bowed low and pushed Jackson toward the Tragically Normals' table.

I watched him sit next to Erin and kiss her on the cheek. She caught me staring and shot me a look that would haunt me forever.

I had arrived at the Potsdam Public Library for our first study session to find Matt slumped at a wooden table by the teen fiction, gazing out the window toward the railroad track that ran along the river. He was in his usual white shirt, and his arms were tan and firm, probably from lifting bales of hay down at the Farm 'n' Feed.

I plunked my tote bag of notebooks on the table. "It's not that bad."

"Yeah, it's bad. Anyway, thanks for doing this." He reached into his pocket and handed me a twenty while giving my lace minidress the once-over. "Still in your funeral garb despite the heat?"

"It's never too hot and humid for black."

"Uh huh. And what, pray tell, is that thing?" he asked, pointing to my neck.

I fingered the necklace I'd found in a secondhand store, a really cool cameo of Persephone on an intricate gold chain. "She's the goddess of death."

"Of course."

That's when I figured we'd better get down to business before things turned nasty. I decided to start with the Puritans; if a strange religious cult of floating functioning alcoholics didn't capture his interest, nothing would.

However, ten minutes into our session, while I attempted to explain the historical precedent of the Mayflower Compact, he was already doodling a boat on his otherwise spotless white notebook page. I gave up and turned over my notes, highlighting which ones were important for the exam. Then I sat back and watched him copy.

He was left-handed.

"What are you staring at?" he asked.

"No need for alarm, but, statistically, left-handers have a lifespan that's two to nine years shorter than right-handers."

Matt flipped the page and squinted at my section on the Plymouth colony. "Is that true?"

"Maybe. Accidents, lower immunity, something having to do with the brain. Makes sense, I suppose." I'd wanted to make him squirm, but he was so nonchalant, I found myself slipping into lame humor. "Either that or you guys keep poking yourselves in the eyes with scissors."

He didn't crack a smile, just kept copying my stuff. "Death is your thing, isn't it? That's why you like history, because everyone's dead."

"Damn straight," I said. "The dead are awesome. They don't give you back talk or interrupt. They never leave you hanging, and they're the best listeners ever. You got a problem? Talk it over with the dead."

A train approached in the evening glow, chugging up the track. A few figures were perched on top, legs dangling over the cars. Freight-hoppers. I'd seen them jump aboard before, running next to the train as it climbed the slight incline, grabbing a side ladder, and then, in one swift, heart-stopping moment, leaping from the ground onto the car, praying that a foot didn't get caught under the wheels.

Aaron Plunkett, a stoner dropout a few years ahead of us in school, used to regularly freight-hop out of Potsdam until he tried it while high, tripped on his shoelaces, and got sucked underneath. I can recall the wail of the sirens erupting around fifth period and everyone rushing to see, word spreading like wildfire that someone had gotten cut in two, a guy with frizzy blond hair who matched Aaron's description.

Later, Sara and I had gone down to the tracks to check out the dark-maroon bloodstains on the tar-coated wooden ties. They're still there to this day.

"James was left-handed," Matt said.

I blinked and returned to the present. "Who's James?"

"My twin." Matt went back to my notes. "You'd like him. He's dead."

Matt turned out to be the Caesar of slacker students: He came. He copied. He left.

He was never late, but he never stayed a minute past eight, either. He did the assigned reading and dutifully answered the questions at the end of each chapter, but didn't brim with academic enthusiasm. And when Erin called or texted, as she tended to do constantly despite our regular study schedule, Matt would glance at the text and put the phone on mute.

This drove me crazy. Not Erin's texting—though that was definitely annoying—but Matt's refusal to enjoy any aspect of learning. Every once in a while I'd see a spark and get excited, like when he drew parallels between America's westward push and Karl Marx's theory that capitalism needed to expand in order to survive. (And we hadn't even covered Communist theory yet.) Once he correctly explained the vast differences between the Republican party of Lincoln's era and its current incarnation.

I was impressed.

Then, just when I was sure we were about to experience an Annie Sullivan/Helen Keller breakthrough, the well went dry and Matt reverted to his old self.

"Is this going to be on the exam?" he'd ask. "Because I don't see the point of going over something if it's not."

Sigh.

I even tried getting him out of the library to the cemetery, where I hoped secluded privacy amid a lush green setting might serve as inspiration. All it inspired was vague rambling and seemingly pointless conjectures.

He would lie in the grass with his shirt off, a hand resting casually on his bare, tanned washboard abs, eyes closed, and start going off about the most random things, like whether squirrels have inner GPSs or why if the sun's rays were powerful enough to burn our rods and cones, how come we were able to exist in radiation at all? He worried out loud that a nuclear war was likely in our lifetime. This was quickly followed by a random musing: Could guys technically be virgins? But as soon as I tried to answer that bizarre question, he was off on another tangent: Had the three-point shot in basketball really been invented to help white players score? Also, was it true parakeets could be poisoned by avocados?

It was exhausting.

On rare occasions, he would brighten when he mentioned his baby nephew, the son of his older half sister, Susan, who lived in Illinois. Other than casual references to his father's strict rules against partying, he didn't talk about his parents much except to say that his mother worked at the DMV and liked to crochet, and that when his dad wasn't coaching high school football, he did construction. They watched a lot of football on TV.

He never spoke of James again, much to my disappointment.

One day, we had just finished a session on Henry Ford and the automobile's effect on American culture when I let it slip that I didn't have my license. Matt sat on the tomb of Arthur Waxman in the blistering August heat as the cicadas buzzed and gaped in awe.

"You don't know how to drive?"

I shrugged. "Not really."

"But you're going to be a senior. What the . . . ?"

There were plenty of lies at my disposal—the family

car was a hearse that got lousy gas mileage and was hard to park, the environment could do with a little less air pollution, thank you, walking was good exercise, etc. Instead, I went with the truth.

"I took driver's ed and I have my permit, but my mother won't let me use the car." There. Done. "Now, we really should try to squeeze in . . ."

"Your mother won't *let* you?" Matt scoffed. "What are you, six?"

Obviously, he was not going to be satisfied until I explained the situation. I closed my book and let him have it.

"Look. When you work in the funeral business, you go to the scenes of a lot of car crashes," I said, relishing the shock I was about to induce. "My mother has actually had to shovel people off the road. *Shovel*, Matt." I made a shoveling motion. "As in *scrape*."

He remained impassive. "So?"

Was he for real? Human remains splattered on the pavement were about the grossest thing ever. "The woman's been traumatized. Do you have any idea what it's like driving with her? She grips the door handle and smashes an invisible brake over and over. It's impossible to rack up forty hours with her sitting next to me. We'd kill each other."

He ran a finger under his lower lip. "All right,

starting next week, I'll pick you up in my truck and we'll clock some hours."

I was speechless. Then again, how else was I going to rack up the necessary hours demanded by the DMV? "I don't suppose your truck is automatic."

He reeled in offense. "Do I look like a wuss?"

"I can't do it, then. I tried once with Boo's Honda and nearly broke the clutch."

"I don't care. You've got to learn standard," he said, placing his hand on mine. "Every girl should."

His hand was warm and his fingers, I noticed, were long, like an artist's. Matt didn't seem to think anything of letting his hand linger there and I didn't dare pull away.

"Why girls?" I asked, acting as if guys like him held my hand every day.

Matt's gaze met mine. I'd never realized before how mesmerizing his eyes were, slightly almond shaped and a deep brown, framed by surprisingly feminine lashes.

"Because guys are dicks, that's why. You don't want to be leaving a party with some drunken asshat behind the wheel just because you can't shift."

He had me at "guys are dicks."

Alas, even the most sensible plans can turn out to be failures. Three days later I was behind the wheel of

Matt's blue pickup truck in a deserted church parking lot, ready to explode. Driving sucked. Stick shift really sucked. Truck stick shift could go . . .

"Swearing's not necessary, Graves," Matt said, smiling. "Cool down, and this time, as you raise your foot off the clutch, step on the gas in an even motion."

Hot, bothered, and totally frustrated by this stupid, stupid system, I blew a stray strand of hair off my sweaty cheek, gripped the steering wheel, and did my best to ease my foot off the clutch. But either I was releasing too soon or not gassing it fast enough, because the truck lurched, bucked violently, and stalled.

I sat back. "I hate this."

Matt yanked up the parking brake to stop our forward roll. "No, you don't. You *want* to hate this. Soon you will love shifting and yearn to go zero to sixty in under five."

"Never. I give up. Anyway, what we're doing is illegal. Technically, I'm supposed to be accompanied by a licensed driver who's at least twenty-one. You're seventeen."

"Eighteen," Matt corrected, adding with a twist of his lips, "and don't worry. You're with me. Membership in the Matt Club has its privileges."

"Oh, please. Because you're the Potsdam Panthers' football hero?"

"Don't get pissy. Now, seriously, let's give it another go. Once you get the hang of shifting, you'll never forget it. Like learning how to ride a bike."

Another miserable childhood experience. "Maybe you should drive," I said. "I've lost interest."

"Not so fast. I have another idea."

Unsnapping his seat belt, he got out and jogged around to my side, opening the door and sliding in. I scooted over, glad to once again be a passenger. Then he raised the steering column, pushed back the seat and patted his shorts. "Hop on."

I gawked at his bare knees and snorted. "You have got to be kidding."

"It's the only way you'll learn. I did it with my dad. I was seven, but, you know, better late than never."

"You honestly want me to sit on your lap?"

"And put your feet over mine. That way you'll get the feel of how and when to release the clutch."

I'd get a feel for a lot more than that, I thought, flustered by the images racing through my mind. "It won't work."

He arched an eyebrow. "Wait. If you think this is my lame attempt to make a move . . ."

"No. Geez. Matt. *No.*" Though that was exactly what I'd been thinking.

". . . because if I wanted to make a move, Graves, I

just would. I don't need a trick."

"I never said you were trying to trick me. That was the furthest thing from my mind."

He grinned. "Then why are you blushing?"

I slapped my cheeks in horror. "I'm not blushing. In case you haven't noticed, it's ninety degrees in this truck."

"Okay, well, I'm not moving until you give this a shot." He shrugged. "You can sit there being weird or you can relax and give it a try."

"Fine. We'll do it your way." Anything to wipe off that smirk. Wiggling over, I squeezed my hips under the steering wheel and perched myself on his knees. "There. Satisfied?"

"Almost." With both hands around my waist, he slowly pulled me into him and positioned me so my back was solidly against his chest. I was acutely aware that my flimsy cotton sundress was the only material separating my legs from his lightly hairy, rock-hard thighs. When he reached around to grab the steering wheel, my heart dropped five stories.

"All righty then. Left foot over left foot. Right over right. You put your hand on the shift." I put my hand on the shift. "Follow my lead."

He closed his hand over mine. My stomach clenched as I registered the warmth of his body.

The truck started and Matt murmured into my ear, "You okay?"

I swallowed. "Yup."

"Clutch is on the left. Gas on the right."

"I know that."

"Do you? From the way you just stalled, I wasn't sure."

I elbowed him in the chest.

"Hey, hey, hey. No need for violence. Now, pay attention."

He lifted his left foot and simultaneously depressed the right. The truck took off gradually and I noticed that Matt had leaned more on the gas than I had. So that's what I'd been doing wrong. I'd been too hesitant to give it juice.

We revved the engine and then I said, "Shift!" remembering to pull the stick into second after he stepped on the clutch. Heading down the service road, out of the parking lot, I moved into third without his reminder.

"Excellent!" he said, pushing my hair out of his face, his fingers trailing along the back of my neck.

He has a girlfriend, I reminded myself.

"The engine's straining. Got to get it up to fourth," he said. "There are monkeys on YouTube better at this than you are, Graves."

That did it. My nervousness and the image of

YouTube monkeys sent me into an uncontrollable spasm of hysterics. I lifted my feet and in doing so accidentally kicked Matt's off the pedals, causing the truck to jerk with a shudder and stall. My head nearly went through the windshield.

Matt shifted into neutral and slammed the brake. "What's wrong with you? You were doing fine."

I fell off his lap onto the passenger seat and kept on laughing. I couldn't help it.

"Have you no dignity?" He placed a hand on his hip and feigned shock at my exposed, bare, tanned legs, which he was openly admiring.

"Rude!" I said, blushing again as I smoothed down the skirt of my dress and sat up.

"Those are not half bad. If you didn't always keep them hidden in that funeral garb of yours, you'd probably get more action."

"Shut up. I get plenty of action," I lied.

"With who? Eric Pienkowski?"

Low blow. Eric was one of those cocky nerds who went on and on about the advantages of PCs over Macs, as if anyone cared. He'd also been my lab partner in Chem, which Matt kept trying to turn into something more.

I slapped my hand over his mouth. "Drop the Eric Pienkowski stuff."

Matt licked my palm until I yanked off my hand and wiped it on the seat. "Ew!"

"That's what you get for trying to shut me up." He turned the ignition and took a left toward downtown and the library.

My damp hand was coated with small white hairs. "This truck is so gross. Don't you ever clean it?"

"Relax, Martha Stewart. Erin's dog, Sparkle, was riding shotgun yesterday. Guess she's shedding."

It so figured that Erin had a dog named Sparkle, no doubt a yippy shih tzu with a rhinestone collar. "What kind is it, a little fluff ball?"

"A little fluff ball that can take your head off. It's an Akita, nastiest canine on the planet. Fortunately, she likes me."

We drove through depressed downtown Potsdam, past the Dollar General and Salabsky's Beverages with its neon Yuengling sign, past Twice Is Nice, a store selling used furniture, and Victoria's Attic, the second-hand/antique store where I'd found the Persephone necklace.

Matt glanced out his side window and groaned. "You get one place to grow up, and this is the card we drew." He flicked his fingers toward the old Wool-worth, its windows soaped and boarded. "Lucky us."

"What's wrong with it?" Not that I didn't have

criticisms of my own about Potsdam; I was just curious to hear his take.

"The air smells like stale beer, for starters." He rolled down the window, sniffed, and then coughed as the pungent stench wafted into the truck. "Everything here is dying. Or already dead. There's no place to go, nothing to do. The day after graduation, I'm outta here and never coming back."

"Where to?"

He slouched against the truck door, one arm dangling over the steering wheel. "The whole world, I guess. Everywhere."

"Everywhere is a pretty big place. Do you have a starting point?"

"I don't know. Alaska, maybe. My uncle has a connection with a guy who runs a salmon boat and is looking for gillnetters. Good money in that. You could make eight thousand in just a summer, easy."

Interesting. Until he brought up Alaska, I'd pictured Matt as the typical jock whose best years would be playing for Penn State. After that, it would be a mid-level job at the brewery managing inventory, a pretty but dissatisfied wife, two kids playing Little League, and on the rare occasion, a reunion with his frat brothers, where he'd get totally wasted.

"With eight grand, I could go anywhere, cross the

Bering Strait to Siberia, hike through China and check out Thailand," he continued. "Then, I'd really like to get to India and see sunrise at the Taj Mahal. I hear it's a very spiritual experience."

My eyebrows lifted. Was this the same Matt Houser who couldn't have cared less about the Transcendentalists' effect on American culture?

"You seem shocked," he said when we stopped at the light.

"Not shocked." I hunted for the right word that wouldn't offend his precious male ego. "*Confused.* What happened to 'I've got to pass US History so I can play football'?"

"Technically, I still have to pass so I won't sit on the bench." The light turned green and he took a left toward the library. "I love football, but if I had it my way, I'd drop out now and head west. I want my life to be different than what everyone's got planned for me, Graves. I want to be *free*."

That word hung in the air between us, potent with meaning.

"You're already free," I said. "You're eighteen and a boy. You can do whatever you want."

Matt threw an arm over the back of the seat and parallel parked into a space one block from the library, completing with one smooth move a maneuver that would have taken me fourteen tries. Then he killed the engine, removed his keys, and said abruptly, "I can't."

"Can't what?"

"Do what I want."

"Sure you can." I lifted my book bag from the floor. Like everything else in this truck, it was covered with Sparkle's white hair. "Why can't you?"

"Because." He stared straight ahead, his expression vacant.

I followed his gaze to the library, where a girl sat on the steps, wearing a green tank top and shorts, her red hair pulled into a tight ponytail, her arms folded. Waiting.

For us.

"Uh oh," I said.

Matt rubbed his brow. "Shit."

"Want me to explain that you were only teaching me how to drive?"

His eyebrows shot up. "Are you serious? No offense, but Erin thinks you're trying to . . . you know . . ." He bowed his head shyly.

Already I could feel the blood rushing to my cheeks. "No. I don't know. *What?*"

He exhaled. "Hook up. With me."

I flushed with outrage. Talk about ego. Erin automatically assumed that every girl—even, apparently,

Matt's parentally approved tutor—lusted after her boyfriend. "Well, I'm not."

"I know that. But it doesn't matter." Matt lifted his head and turned sideways. "You've got to understand. Erin's not like you. Not at all."

I slunk down in the seat in case she recognized Matt's truck. "What does that mean?"

"It means she can't just brush stuff off and go with the flow. I don't know how to describe it, but sometimes I worry she's such a perfectionist that if everything doesn't turn out exactly the way she wants, she might hurt herself."

I was stunned. There was nothing about Erin Donohue that seemed the least bit self-destructive.

For the most part, Erin *was* perfect. Teachers adored her. Guys were intimidated, and most girls wanted to be her.

"You want to give me an example?" I said.

Matt ran a finger under his lower lip, thinking. "Okay, like, last spring after junior prom I suggested that we might want to take a break for the summer, and . . ."

"And what?"

"It wasn't good."

"Oh." I waited for him to elaborate, but he didn't. Possibly because a tall, thin guy with long, black hair bouncing on his shoulders was jaywalking across Main Street with a purpose. He was Alex Bone, aka Stone Bone, one of the weirdest dudes ever to grace the halls of Potsdam High.

He'd been a senior when Sara and I had been mere freshmen, so he seemed scarier than he probably was. Though his penchant for wearing scruffy dusters and making videos about how much the school sucked didn't help. For that reason, Sara nicknamed him Mr. Columbine and profiled him as Most Likely to Take Out the Cafeteria.

He scared the crap out of us, but apparently he didn't have the same effect on Erin, who suddenly jumped up and ran down the steps to give him a great big hug.

"What's she doing with Stone Bone?" Matt asked, leaning forward.

We watched as Alex touched his hands together prayerfully and bowed. Erin did the same. Alex reached into his back pocket and pulled out a book. Erin took it and clasped it to her chest before kissing his cheek. Alex touched his cheek with his fingertips and brought them to his lips. There was something ritualistic in their mannerisms—intimate, yet almost orchestrated.

Then he backed up and jogged across the street,

pausing to look at her affectionately before pulling open the door of the Pots & Cups Café. I remembered hearing somewhere that he was a barista. Struck me as odd job for a guy who couldn't stand people. Erin, meanwhile, had climbed back up the steps of the library, where she sat reading Alex's gift.

"I better find out what that was all about," Matt said, getting out and closing the truck door softly so she wouldn't twirl around to see me sitting in Sparkle's shotgun spot. Leaning in the window, he said, "I think we should skip our study session today. Okay?"

"Sure. Absolutely." I didn't want to face Erin anyway.

"I'll drive you home. Just give me a minute."

I nodded and let him go. After twenty minutes of watching the two of them talk on the library steps, I slipped out with my book bag and walked the four miles.

SEVEN

"Hey, Graves." Matt shook my shoulder. "Wake up."

"I don't want to," I whispered.

"You've got to. I need you."

I could sense him weighing down the foot of my bed. Though my eyes were closed, I saw his white T-shirt and the rounded contours of his quarterback shoulders in the morning dusk. Oddly enough, his hair was longish, which was how I knew it was only a dream. During football season, he wore it super short.

I opened my eyes and let reality sink in. My room was empty, the garden window closed. Matt had never been here. He didn't care about me.

"Goddammit," I whispered, and turned on my

phone to see if by chance he'd written during the night. A bazillion texts filled the screen.

-Erin would be alive if not 4 u.

-You should pay for what you did.

-I don't know how you can stand to live with yourself!

-You should be the one dead—not her.

The phone fell from my hand as I reeled from all the vitriol. This was a whole new level of hostility. For some reason, the Tragically Normals—at least, I assumed it was the Tragically Normals—had apparently decided to lay the blame for Erin's death on me.

I leaned over to get my phone and, bracing for the worst, forced myself to read the texts again. They originated from Pinger, which meant they'd be almost impossible to trace. With a shaky thumb, I deleted every one. *Bing. Bing. Bing.* And then I called Sara.

"Hey!" she answered cheerily. "I was just about to call you. I might be a little late because—"

"What the hell is going on?"

"Huh?"

I described the texts, right down to the last breathtaking zinger: *Lily Graves should be IN the grave.* "It's like suddenly I'm under attack for no reason."

"Okay, okay. Take a deep breath."

I took a deep breath.

"First of all, *you* have done nothing wrong. Don't be manipulated. Second of all, those texts violate the school's bullying policy. I spent half the night lying awake and strategizing how best to bring them down without making you look like a whining snitch."

Sara was already aware of the rumors? "But why are they ganging up on me all of a sudden?"

"I'll tell you in the car. Just take a shower, get a cup of coffee, pull up your big-girl panties, and stay calm. All right?"

"I guess. Though I still don't . . ."

"And whatever you do, do not go online. No Twitter. No Facebook."

Facebook? Who went on Facebook anymore?

"Meet you at seven thirty-ish. I might be a little late. Okay?"

"Okay." I felt slightly better knowing that whatever it was, Sara had my back. I pressed end and there was a buzz. Another message.

I. Hate. You.

I wondered if that one had been sent by Matt.

Following Sara's advice, I slid out of bed into the cold morning and dragged myself to the kitchen to brew a pot of coffee. Meanwhile, I dialed up the thermostat, fetched the newspaper off the top step, and let out our cat, Mitzy.

Coffee in hand, I opened the French doors off our kitchen and stepped onto the brick patio. The air was chilly and scented with autumn decay: rotting pumpkins, moldy flowers, and other glorious dead things. As each bright ray of the rising sun touched the remaining red and gold leaves, they fluttered to the ground in a silent rain. It was so pretty and bittersweet that for a brief moment I forgot about the awaiting horde of hatemongers.

"Good morning!" my mother announced as her heels clicked onto the patio, nearly scaring me out of my skin. Being Ruth B. Graves, she was already showered, suited, and ready for work, right down to her tasteful nude lip gloss and tightly wound chignon. "You're up early."

"Noisy garbage truck." There was no point in telling her about my dreams about Matt or the hate bombs. It would only make her fret, and already the worry lines between her eyes were turning permanent.

She placed her coffee and iPad on the glass table and took a seat on a wrought-iron chair before scrolling through the morning paper to the obituary section. Mom read the obits like stockbrokers checked the morning overseas markets, part and parcel of staying up on the competition.

"Do I dare ask what you're going to wear this morning?" she asked without looking up.

The eternal question. "What I always wear." And before she could object, I said, "Please don't argue. It's going to be a stressful day, and I need all the support I can get."

Mom loved giving support. I think it was a major reason why she took over my father's business after he died—so she had permission to hold hands and coo, "There, there."

"All right," she conceded reluctantly. "Go get dressed. Sara will be here any minute."

A half hour later, I reappeared in my favorite body-hugging black dress with bell sleeves. My shoulder-length hair, the shade and silkiness of ravens' feathers, hung steel straight, with a strip of blue for pizazz. A pair of Doc Martens added the necessary heft.

The only thing missing was the Persephone cameo, my absolute favorite accessory that I had somehow lost swimming last summer. Matt may have poked fun at it, but I loved the Persephone myth—how she came to rule the Underworld yet also remain a loyal daughter. As stupid as it might seem, I felt stronger with Persephone around my neck, and I suspected that this was going to be one of those days when I would need all the strength I could muster.

Mom lifted her gaze from the iPad and emitted a sigh of maternal suffering. "Really, Lily? Today when you're going to police headquarters you can't compromise on—"

"Mom . . . ," I warned.

She went back to reading. "I'm just saying."

A crunch of gravel followed by a quick beep in the driveway announced Sara's arrival.

"Got to go!" With a kiss on her forehead, I sailed out the door and into the refuge of the McMartins' blue Mercedes.

Sara greeted me with an approving assessment. "Good. That sends the right message." She waved to the chrome coffee mug in the cup holder, the one we called the Cup o' Bling because it was covered in plastic diamonds. "I made you a cappuccino before I left. Three shots of espresso."

"Thanks," I whispered, taking a deep sip.

Sara brewed the absolute best cup of coffee. She started learning the tricks of the barista trade when she was young, around eleven, after her mother stopped getting out of bed to make breakfast in the mornings. Dr. Ken was always at the hospital by five for rounds, so it was up to Sara to rouse her brother, Brandon, and make sure he washed his face, brushed his teeth, and didn't leave for school in his Pokémon pj's.

Sara cut her teeth on instant, moved to drip, and eventually mastered the frothy cappuccino, complete with swirls of steamed milk in the shape of a heart, like they do down at the café.

"Okay," I said, curling my fingers around the warm cup. "Brief me, counselor."

Her gaze flitted to the rearview. "I first heard the rumors yesterday when Dad and I brought a casserole over to the Donohues. They only had, like, twenty there on the counter already."

I could have told her that. Soup-based casseroles were synonymous with death. Campbell's should consider placing a picture of the Grim Reaper on its cream of mushroom.

"Anyway, Kate Kline was there with her family too." Sara stopped at a crosswalk to let a group of little kids pass, their backpacks bouncing as they marched to school with amusing seriousness. I had a sudden image of Kate and Erin at that age, prancing into second grade with their own matching pink Britney Spears backpacks, queens of the class even then.

The crossing guard waved us onward and Sara continued. "As soon as we were alone, she grabbed me by the arm and started grilling me about you and Matt."

"*Me and Matt?* What's there to know? For the thousandth time, we're friends. Nothing more."

"Not to the TNs. They're convinced you two were cheating behind Erin's back."

My jaw dropped. Matt and I hadn't so much as held hands or kissed or . . . anything.

Well, that wasn't exactly technically true, I thought guiltily, thinking back to a couple of times when we nearly crossed the line.

"Here's what else," Sara said, flicking another glance at the rearview. "Kate got that stuff about you and Matt from Erin on Saturday, the day she died. That's why everyone's putting the blame on you, Lil. Don't get me wrong. It's totally unfair. But that's the deal."

Suddenly, I couldn't breathe. It was as if someone had socked me in the solar plexus. Cramps radiated through my middle, and I had to lean over to stop them. I wanted to stay that way forever, invisible and hidden, until my existence was forgotten.

"You okay?" Sara asked.

I gripped my waist and tried sitting up. "Yeah. I don't know what's wrong. Nerves."

"That's why I didn't tell you. I knew you'd get upset, especially since—"

"Erin didn't kill herself."

Sara's eyes went wide. "Excuse me?"

My mother would have had a fit if she'd found

out I was violating her specific order not to tell Sara, but I was sick of lying to my best friend. Besides, this suicide business had gone on long enough. "She was murdered."

Sara slammed on the brakes just as the light turned red. "Where'd you get that?"

"I saw an internal memo Perfect Bob faxed to Mom. Then Mom confirmed yesterday when she told me I had to go to headquarters today to get my cheek swabbed so they could separate out my DNA from whoever else's is under Erin's fingernails."

"Whoa! Whoa! Whoa!" Sara gripped her right temple. "Information overload. Back up and tell me everything from the beginning."

So I told her about snooping in Mom's office and seeing the fax—conveniently omitting the part about Bob's instructions to keep me away from Matt. Then I explained about the buccal smear and how Bob had convinced Mom that the test didn't mean I was a suspect, though I couldn't help feeling like one.

Sara was so stunned she didn't even notice the light had turned green until a car behind us leaned on the horn, whereupon she flipped him the bird and floored it. We sped along silently for a bit. I lowered the window for some fresh air, and then she said in a dull monotone, "Why would anyone have murdered Erin?"

"That's the million-dollar question, isn't it?"

Chilled, I raised the window and turned my attention to Sara. All color had drained from her already alabaster complexion and her lips were a pale blue. For a crime junkie who spent her free hours glued to *Investigation Discovery*, her worst nightmare had just come true: a girl her age in her neighborhood had been murdered in her own upstairs bathroom while her parents had been out of town.

Creepy things like this weren't supposed to happen in Potsdam, especially not in the supposedly safe and suburban Pinewoods development where Sara's and Erin's parents ponied up for monthly security on the naïve assumption that something as flimsy as an electronic gate could protect their kids from evil.

"Three streets away, Lil," she said, her voice hoarse. "The same railroad track runs through our backyards. The killer could have been freight-hopping. Or maybe he'd been stalking her from the woods and just waiting for the moment when her parents were out of town to get her unaware."

"I know. I know. It's freaky."

The knuckles of Sara's right hand were white against the black steering wheel. "Do they have any idea who it might have been?"

"I don't think so." In an attempt to calm her, I

added softly, "According to the fax, there was no sign of forced entry, which means most likely it wasn't a freight-hopper or some stalker, but that Erin probably knew her killer."

Matt. I immediately shook this thought out of my head.

"Or," Sara added, "he's a supersmart psychopathic serial killer like Israel Keyes, who lived in Alaska and traveled to the lower forty-eight states and rented cars under various aliases so there'd be no connections to the victims he picked at random. God knows how many people he killed before he did himself in."

I had to resist the temptation to roll my eyes. Sara needed to curb her TV habit or it was going to warp her mind, if it hadn't already.

Sara hooked an abrupt right into someone's driveway and scrutinized her driver's side mirror.

"What's wrong?" I asked, thinking maybe she needed a chance to pull it together.

"I want this jerk behind me to pass. He's been on my tail since Evergreen."

We both turned around to see a nondescript gray Ford sedan. It stopped, waited, and then pulled a U-ey, speeding off in the opposite direction with a screech of its tires, kicking up a cloud of dust.

Sara and I exchanged glances. "You don't think . . . ,"
she said.

"That he was following you? Nah."

"Then why did he . . . ?"

"Maybe he was lost. You're just being paranoid."

"Yeah, maybe." Sara flicked on her turn signal and
headed out to the road.

We didn't say another word until we got to school.

Potsdam Regional High was built in the 1970s
when three towns merged into one school district
and bought up a bunch of farmland for a new, mod-
ern facility. The building itself was an eyesore, the
brainchild of the open-concept system, when it was
fashionable to teach in classrooms without walls.
That lasted for all of five minutes before they rolled
in paper-thin temporary partitions that were never
replaced, so what was being taught one room over
was crystal clear.

My main gripe, however, was the lack of windows. The same professionals who decided it was
a good idea to remove walls also thought the same
applied to glass. Supposedly this was to keep students from being distracted. The result was that,
unless you were in the cafeteria (windows galore)
or in the atrium (skylights above), Potsdam High

seemed an awful lot like a high-security correctional facility.

But that day there were other reasons to call it a prison.

"Are they serious?" Sara asked as we approached the front entrance, where not one but four Potsdam police officers waited to greet us with wands and metal detectors.

Annoyed students rummaged through their backpacks to remove laptops, iPads, phones, and anything else that might set off alarms.

"Was there a bomb threat?" I asked a chinless patrolman, who scrutinized my outfit with a disapproving scowl.

"Do you have any knives, guns, weapons of any sort?" he responded, ignoring my question as he pawed through my bag.

"Not unless you count the pins in the voodoo doll."

He didn't even crack a smile. "Step forward, please, and hold out your arms."

It was humiliating, being scanned in public. I don't know why I considered it such an invasion of privacy, but I did, especially when he ran the wand up and down my legs and across my crotch.

Cleared for education, Sara and I slipped on our shoes and gathered our stuff. The whole experience was decidedly Orwellian.

"This is because of Erin, you know," I said as we crossed the atrium.

"Kind of gives credence to your theory that she was murdered."

"You had doubts?"

Sara stopped. "Lil. This is the Potsdam PD we're dealing with here. Did you take a good look at those dudes? The crossing guards we just passed are more qualified."

Over her shoulder, I spied a sheet of pink poster board that had been tacked up outside of Guidance on Monday so people could write their condolences to Erin. Every inch was covered in ink.

MISS YOU!

LOVE YOU!

I KEEP LOOKING FOR YOUR SMILE AT PRACTICE.

(DON'T FORGET SKITTLE BUMPS!)

MY HEART IS DARK KNOWING YOU HAVE GONE.

I CAN'T BELIEVE IT'S TRUE.

I CAN'T STOP CRYING.

PLEASE, NO. NO. NO. NO.

There were many random lyrics from various songs, too many from "The Wind Beneath My Wings." But it was the dedication at the bottom that stopped me short.

I WILL ALWAYS LOVE YOU, E. PEACE.

It was signed simply *M*, which I knew had to be Matt. He was back.

Picking up a Sharpie, I hastily scribbled *Rest in peace, Erin. I'll find him*, and signed it *Lily G.*

Sara stooped to read it. "You meant you're going to find the killer, right?"

"Yeah."

"Because people might take that the wrong way."

"Good."

They were waiting for me upstairs. Blond and petite Cheyenne Day, dark-haired and almond-eyed Allie Woo, and their new queen, Kate Kline, Erin's presumed successor.

An ambush.

"There she is," Kate announced as Allie and Cheyenne whipped out their cells to document in texts and photos whatever was about to go down.

Kate was shorter than I was by a good five inches. But what she lacked in height, she more than made up for in self-righteous indignation. Below the adorable widow's peak that defined the part of her straight brown hair were equally pointy eyebrows that highlighted her mesmerizing blue eyes. Guys in school were secretly intrigued by Kate but few asked her out because they felt intimidated. I never understood that—before.

"Excuse me," I said, gesturing to my locker, which she was blocking.

Kate didn't move. "I bet you're glad Erin's dead."

"Don't be stupid, Kate."

"Don't be lying, Lily. You've been jealous of her since elementary school."

Not jealous. More like resentful of the way she made fun of Sara's disability and my family's profession, as if we were subhuman for not being symmetrical specimens whose parents worked in the brewery's headquarters.

A teacher passed by and wished us a good morning. I used the reprieve to spin my combination—25, 9, 33—while Sara positioned herself on my other side, just in case things got out of hand.

The teacher disappeared. The locker popped open. Kate slammed it shut. "I hope you're satisfied."

"With what?" I stuck my finger in the handle and opened it again. Sara leaned against the door so Kate couldn't close it.

"*With what?*" Kate shook her head so her hair rippled like a Pantene commercial. "With pushing Erin to the edge, that's with what. She'd be alive today if it weren't for you."

Sara rolled her eyes. "Oh, please."

After depositing my heavy calculus book on the top shelf, I closed the locker and gave the combination lock a quick flick. "I didn't do anything to Erin. With all due respect to the dead, whatever she told you about Matt and me is wrong."

"It's not what she said, it's what I *saw*," Kate spat back. "Those scratches you gave her? You are one sick puppy to do that to her."

Sara dropped her jaw. "Lil, you can't let her get away with that."

No kidding. "Um, for the record," I said, "Erin attacked *me*."

"Another lie!" Kate smiled triumphantly at Cheyenne and Allie. "*For the record*, Lily, I went to Erin's house Saturday evening, since she didn't meet me at the game like she was supposed to and she wasn't answering her phone. Matt had just broken up with her—"

"Because of you," Allie chimed in—a mistake, because this was Kate's show. Kate glared at her reprovingly. Allie retreated.

"Anyway, when I got there," Kate continued, "I

found Erin on the couch, a total mess. I asked what happened and she told me that you'd finally managed to turn Matt against her just so you could get him for yourself. You broke her heart, Lily. She killed herself because of you."

Sara said, "You don't know anything."

I sucked in a breath because, although I appreciated Sara's defense, I didn't want her to blow it so soon. The murder theory was still supposed to be a secret. If it got out via us instead of the cops, Mom would kill me.

"Sara . . . ," I said, smiling. "Remember?"

"Screw it, Lil. Kate's talking out of her ass."

Kate sneered. "Shut up, Shrinky Dink."

Instinctively, I lifted my hand, this close to slapping her hard enough to send that stupid adorable widow's peak of hers to the back of her head. She hadn't dared call Sara "Shrinky Dink" since I overheard her whisper it to Erin when Sara missed an assist in volleyball back in middle school gym class. It had been worth detention just to see the fear in Kate's eyes as I pushed her against the gym wall and threatened to mess up her widow's peak forever if she ever mocked my best friend again. Ms. Seidel had to forcibly drag me away, I was so enraged.

"Yeah, go ahead and hurt me," Kate said defiantly. "Just like you hurt Erin."

Sara lowered her eyes, a signal that I should lower my hand. Reluctantly, I did.

"You're an awful person, Kate," I said. "Selfish, vain, and cruel."

"Like I care," Kate replied with a defiant lift of her chin. "Insulting *your* friend hardly compares to what you did to *my* friend, Lily." Kate lightly raked her own cheeks. "I saw the blood."

Bull. I hadn't even broken skin. Rolling up my own sleeves, I thrust out my arm to reveal the scabbed streaks. "Yeah, well shortly before you found Erin sobbing on the couch playing the victim, she'd attacked me in the graveyard. Look!"

All four girls plus Sara leaned in for closer inspection. Then Kate turned to Allie and Cheyenne. "Didn't I tell you guys Erin tried to defend herself?"

"Unreal," Sara said.

Cheyenne snapped a few shots of my arm. In a matter of seconds, the pictures were circulated throughout the school as proof of my complicity in Erin's supposed suicide.

"It's so like you to trash Erin after she's dead," Kate sing-songed as the second bell rang. "By the way, in case you were wondering, you're on Matt's shit list too."

I swallowed and hugged my books tighter.

"You know what he calls you, Lily?"

Sara gripped my elbow, while I tried desperately to keep my face impassive.

"Pathetic."

I walked off before my tears gave me away.

My class lineup that day was calculus, English lit, physics (in which we had a pop quiz), and World Cultures. So I decided to exercise my prerogative and skip the afternoon to hang out in the school library reading up on handy uses for chicken blood in Haitian death rituals. Besides, the last thing my psyche needed was to be surrounded by my haters. Also, let's be honest—what was the point of sitting through a droning lecture about the European Union when my future was already set in stone? Literally.

After high school, I would major in mortuary science at Center Valley Community College, where Mom got her degree and which conveniently required no more than a 2.5 for admission. There, I'd study anatomy and physiology, embalming theory, mortuary law, and chemistry, as well as the more lucrative "Mortuary Marketing" and the squishier "Understanding the Grieving Process."

"You could teach those professors a thing or two," Boo often said. She was probably right. I highly doubted that most of the esteemed staff of CVCC had read

The Tibetan Book of the Dead from beginning to end or that, by age eight, they had learned never to use the femoral artery as a point of injection for embalming fluid when the cadaver was obese. Always go with the carotid if possible. *Always.*

Unfortunately, Kemple's reptilian brain was too unevolved to grasp the complex logic behind my skipping, and I soon accumulated enough detentions to equal a suspension. I stood my ground—I was going to study what I wanted, when I wanted, and if Kemple had a problem with my "nontraditional" approach to education, then he could kick me out.

He never did. At least, not until I looked up from my chapter on chicken blood potions to see a pair of pale, watery eyes glaring at me over his bifocals.

"There are two gentlemen waiting for you in my office," Kemple's doughy lips mouthed. "I'd like you to come with me."

There was nothing to be had in telling Herr Kemple that I was simply performing my civic duty by talking to the cops. He wouldn't have believed me, anyway.

"So sad about Erin," I said, scurrying after him as we proceeded down the hall.

Kemple said nothing. Nice.

We entered the school office, where even the normally friendly secretary, Mrs. Foy, avoided eye contact as I passed by on my way to Kemple's private quarters. Inside his office, two uniformed police officers rose to attention with lots of crackling leather.

I recognized the chinless one from that morning's security detail. Kemple introduced him as Officer Wohotek; the other was Officer Delray. He tipped his hat politely. I assumed he would be playing the role of good cop.

"I'm going to nip out and check where they are," Kemple said, making a quiet exit.

I wanted to ask who he was checking on, but Officer Wohotek said, "So who are you supposed to be?"

I stared at him blankly.

Delray translated. "Like, who are you being for Halloween?" He waved to my attire. "A vampiress or something?"

"Oh. No." I studied my black lace, having temporarily forgotten that to some people this was not considered normal school wear. "Halloween's tomorrow. This is how I always dress."

Wohotek cracked his knuckles, and Delray said, "Takes all kinds."

After two minutes of awkward standing around, Kemple popped his head in the door. "They're ready."

"Shall we?" Delray asked, placing his hand lightly on my upper left arm while Wohotek secured my right. Then they guided me out the door, and it hit me too late that I had been suckered into an impromptu walk of shame.

But it wasn't until I spied Jackson at the end of the hall in his goofy out-of-season plaid shorts and Adidas sandals that I understood I'd been conned. Next to Jackson was Matt, texting on his phone.

At the sight of him, my feet stopped and my blood froze. All this time wondering how he was, what he was thinking, if it was true he hated me or if that had been just another of Kate Kline's lies. And there he was, within reach.

Jackson nudged Matt, who looked up from his phone and met my gaze, his entire demeanor instantly changing from bored to alert. He seemed surprised and relieved, but also something else: angry.

Wohotek and Delray pulled me forward, but I resisted. If Matt so much as swore, he'd be playing right into their hands. Clearly, Kemple had arranged for him to see me in police custody in an attempt to elicit a reaction, hopefully one that might lead to admission of guilt or, better, a false confession.

We'd been set up.

"Hey!" Matt said. "What's going on? Where are they taking you?"

"It's nothing," I said, trying to smile so he wouldn't worry.

"Doesn't look like nothing." He confronted Wohotek. "You can't just haul her away. She didn't do anything wrong."

"That's for the law to decide," Wohotek said.

At that, Matt lunged toward them like he was on the football field. Delray yanked me away and Wohotek blocked him with a stiff arm. "Hold on there, son. You wouldn't want to do something you'll regret later."

Jackson yelled, "Dude, what are you doing? Are you nuts? You don't mess with the cops over a girl. Let it go."

"Like hell." Matt refused to budge and stood there, ready to bust through Wohotek. "You guys need to back off!"

My heart pretty much snapped in two then.

I said, "Seriously, Matt, it's fine."

But my words were lost in the melee that followed. Kemple, Jackson, and Mr. Quinn, the athletic director, who seemed to have miraculously emerged from nowhere, swarmed on Matt and pinned him to the wall while Delray ushered me into the school lobby.

I didn't have to look back to know he was watching, just as I didn't have to ask if he still cared.

He did.

EIGHT

The buccal smear turned out to be fairly tolerable. A female officer brought me into a back room, where they scanned fingerprints and made me sign a bunch of forms saying I was doing this willingly. Then she ripped open a sealed plastic bag and, with latex gloves, removed a long-handled Q-tip that was swiped along the inside of my cheek. She did that three more times, deposited the swabs in tubes, and we were done.

Mom was there to cosign the paperwork since I was a minor. And Perfect Bob tried to put me at ease in his dorky Boy Scout way by praising me for being a "good girl" and saying how the police department's work would be cut in half if everyone were so cooperative.

"Don't forget that Lily and Erin were friends," Mom said, which the three of us knew was a lie. Bob had been there the night I got back from the graveyard. He saw.

And he didn't forget.

"Would you be willing to give a statement about what happened that evening?" Bob asked, handing me a stick of Trident to remove the cotton-mouth sensation. "We sure could use any assistance you could provide."

I was tempted to ask what the consequences would be if I refused, but there was Mom wringing her hands anxiously, so I said, "Okay."

We were ushered into another room, this one obviously reserved for questioning. It wasn't cinderblock like on Sara's Investigation Discovery reenactments, but the floor was concrete and the heavy wooden chairs were worn. It smelled of ground-in coffee and stale cigarettes from back in the day when smoking was allowed. To add to its whimsical charm, the walls had been painted a bilious yellow with pictures of the governor and the president above the state seal of the Commonwealth of Pennsylvania.

On the other wall was the two-way mirror.

Due to a glaring conflict of interest, Bob couldn't

take my statement. That was the duty of one Detective Joseph Henderson. As in Henderson from the fax I shouldn't have seen. I practically blushed when he entered the room, as if I'd been caught snooping in his underwear drawer.

Bob said, "Take it easy on her, Joe. She's a friend."

Mom couldn't help smiling a little when Bob left on some pretense of having to prepare for a press conference, though I'd have bet my last dollar on him observing from the two-way.

Henderson was a short, squat, potbellied man who made an admirable effort of upholding the poor fashion sense of plainclothes cops. The brown polyester tie with blue dots didn't even make sense with his red-and-blue-striped shirt or the tweed jacket. It was probably a tie he kept in a permanent knot and hung on his office door for fieldwork and office parties.

The three of us took our places, with me at the head of the table and Henderson across from Mom. He asked how the smear went and said that it would drive him nuts to have cotton in his mouth. He could barely stand getting that dry-air spritz at the dentist's.

Mom put her purse in her lap and clutched it, her complexion paler than usual against the black suit she always wore. "This won't take long, I hope," she said, eyeing the fresh set of forms Henderson had produced from a manila folder. "Lily has homework."

"Oh, no. Nothing major," he said, shuffling the papers. "We're just gathering statements." Turning on his digital recorder, he said, "Lily, you are free to leave at any time. Do you understand?"

Meaning, I wasn't under arrest. *Yet.*

The pretense for this meeting was that Henderson simply wanted a statement about what went down with Erin on Saturday evening in the graveyard. And that was how the interview started, but soon he was nosing into my relationship with Erin ("We've had our ups and downs"), and then my observations of Erin's relationship with Matt ("They had their ups and downs"), and finally *my* relationship with Matt.

Mom let out a sigh. "I knew this was where we were headed," she said, dismayed. We'd been there for over an hour already.

"Like I stated at the outset, Mrs. Graves, we can stop the questioning at any point," Henderson said. "You give me the word and we're through."

If we stopped the questioning, it would look fishy. It would appear that Matt and I had something to hide when we didn't.

"It's all right," I said. "I just don't want to get Matt into trouble by accidentally saying something that'll be misinterpreted."

"You don't want to get Matt Houser into trouble, huh?" Henderson's mouth curled cynically. "Yeah, I can see how you wouldn't want nothing bad to happen to him."

From beneath his yellow tablet, he removed another manila file. "Mrs. Graves, what I'm about to show your daughter are crime scene photos. You might want to look away."

Mom had to bite her lower lip to keep from laughing.

"She was *at* the crime scene," I said. "Hell, she did the retrieval."

"Don't swear, Lily!" Mom said sharply, but I could tell that she was pleased. Nothing yanked my mother's chain like a man who dismissed her as a cupcake.

"My apologies. I forgot." Henderson parted his lips to reveal brown cigar- and coffee-stained teeth. "How about you, Lily? These are very upsetting photos."

I knew Mom didn't want it revealed that I helped prep bodies, including Erin's, because she could lose her license for that, so I played coy. "It might be difficult, but I'll do my best."

"Much appreciated." Henderson opened the file with an overly dramatic arc of the arm and slid out the first photo. He was right. The picture was jarring, even for an experienced dead-person handler like myself.

At first, I couldn't even make out Erin, there was so much white on white. It was the pink towel rimmed in red blood that served as the focal point, followed by her eyes. They were glassy and open, turned toward the viewer in an expression of pathetic helplessness. Her glorious copper hair was barely visible behind her face, which was alabaster white aside from two dark-red lines of blood streaming from her nostrils.

I swallowed hard and said, "Poor Erin."

"That's an understatement." Henderson showed me the next, a close-up of her arms, each with its identical vertical incisions.

Whoever did this knew what he was doing. The cuts were right through the arteries, no running into bones or tendons. There was an almost surgical precision that would have been impossible to inflict if Erin had been struggling even slightly.

Could someone else have been holding her down? Maybe *two* other people?

I studied the first photo of the scene. That was another thing. There should have been more blood. But there wasn't. None on the bathtub or walls. Only in the water, on the towel, and on her upper lip. It took at least fifteen minutes to die from slitting your wrists—an unpleasant, extremely painful way to go—and Erin would have certainly been thrashing.

The human heart is capable of pumping one hundred pounds of blood one mile high, and if there are open vessels around, that blood is going to spray everywhere. The only logical explanation for the pristine white tile walls, therefore, was that Erin's heart hadn't been beating when she was cut. Whoever did this to her had killed her first and staged it to make it look like a suicide. Now I understood Henderson's fax and why he requested the crime lab.

We were dealing with a psychopath.

My gaze fell on the glass of clear liquid upright on the bathroom floor, probably the same one I read about in the police report faxed to Mom. Might be a clue.

"Are these pictures really necessary?" Mom asked. "I mean, honestly, Lily has already been traumatized as it is."

"Erin was traumatized, too," Henderson said, tapping the photos. "So how do you feel about Mr. Houser now?"

I sat back. "Matt had nothing to do with this. He wouldn't know how to slice through someone's arms without making a mess. The killer here knew exactly where the radial arteries were in relation to the bone and he wasn't a millimeter off."

Henderson raised an eyebrow. "And you do?"

"I've read a lot of books on anatomy and embalming. We have them around the house from when Mom was getting her mortuary science degree."

"Lily's planning to take over the family business some day," my mother said proudly.

"Really?" Henderson said. "Okay, Lily, then how about you tell me what *you* were doing in the early morning hours of October twenty-eighth?"

Mom jumped up. "You promised this wouldn't be an interrogation."

"It's okay, Mom." Henderson was merely wasting my time and taxpayers' dollars, stupidly targeting Matt and me. But if that was the way he wanted to roll, so be it.

Returning Henderson's bloodshot gaze with my clear one, I said, "I was in my bedroom watching Netflix on my laptop. Around 1:00 a.m., Mom knocked on my door and told me to go to bed."

"That's true," Mom said, lowering herself into the chair. "I woke up and heard her laughing. The girl keeps the hours of a vampire."

Henderson checked his digital recorder and jotted a note. "When did you last hear from Matt Houser, Lily?"

"Friday night. By text."

He nodded to my iPhone resting on the table, muted. "Mind if I take a look?"

I scrolled through my phone messages and let him read Matt's own words in response to my suggestion that he watch my favorite movie, *Local Hero*.

Ur films suck nothing ever happens in them

I responded:

b/c u r a moron, try expanding your brain. the dude from animal house is cute and he has a little bunny.

He wrote:

that he ate. nice.

We exchanged a couple of messages about how he loved any movie with Seth Rogen and then I went to bed.

The following day, I texted this: *You won't believe what happened.* Next to it was the photo of my brutalized arm.

Henderson cringed. "You sent that to him?"

"Yes. Around six on Saturday night."

"And what was his reply?"

"Nothing."

"Did you call him again?" Henderson asked. "Or text?"

"Both. But, like I said . . . nothing."

Mom sniffed triumphantly. "There. Are we through?"

Henderson ignored her. "No personal visits? No rendezvous in the cemetery, perhaps, in your special love-nest tomb?"

How did he know about that? I shot a look at Mom.

"I need your answer verbally," Henderson prodded. "Tape recorder can't pick up a reaction."

"No," I barked.

"All right. No need to shout."

Henderson repeated the order of events twice more and then he closed his tablet. Finally.

But as I pushed back my chair, he said, "Just want to be clear on one thing. You've known Matt since elementary school, but you didn't become close until this summer. Why?"

We'd already been over this. "Because I had to tutor him in US History so he could pass the course and play football, remember?"

"Memory's not what it used to be. I'll get my prompter." He signaled to the two-way mirror, and almost immediately the door flew open and in walked a trim, bald man about my mother's age. Henderson introduced him as Detective Zabriskie from the Pennsylvania State Police, homicide division.

Ah, yes, the PSP backup Henderson had requested in his fax.

With a courteous bow to Mom, Zabriskie whipped around a chair and straddled it, regarding me from behind a pair of steel-framed glasses.

"Nice to meet you, Miss Graves," he said, extending his hand. "Thank you for your time." He clicked a pen and scanned the notes Henderson had just taken on our conversation, riffling through the yellow pages noisily. "We'll try not to keep you much longer. Detective Henderson has done an excellent job, but I need to refresh his memory."

"And we need to get going," Mom said.

Zabriskie tapped the tablet. "This will take only a minute, ma'am. Just to make sure I have the facts right, Miss Graves, starting in July you began tutoring Matt Houser twice a week in US History. Is that correct?"

I understood that a girl had died and they had to be thorough, but this was like beating a dead horse. "That's right."

"What day did Mr. Houser call to request your services, exactly?"

"I don't remember."

Zabriskie waved this away. "No problem. If necessary we can subpoena your phone records. We've already got a court order to get Mr. Houser's."

"Subpoena!" Mom exclaimed. "I'm not very comfortable with how this is going."

Neither was I. If there was a court order to get Matt's phone records, then that meant the cops might already have received a warrant to search his house and car and locker. It meant . . .

"You seriously believe Matt's a suspect," I said, "don't you?"

Zabriskie adjusted his frames. "And you have some objection?"

"You're after the wrong guy. Matt didn't kill anyone and neither did I. All I did was tutor him so he could pass a makeup test and play football. All Matt did was stick with Erin because he was concerned about her mental state. That doesn't exactly sound like a killer to me."

"Uh huh." Zabriskie was unmoved. "By the way, why did Mr. Houser ask you to tutor him when his girlfriend got an A in that class too?"

"His parents thought Erin might be too much of a distraction."

Zabriskie sucked his teeth. "And this is what his parents said to you directly."

"No. I've never even met the Housers."

"So you don't know if they were aware that their son was being tutored to take a makeup exam in history."

This reminded me of how I felt at camp when we played a game where the name of a famous person was taped to my back and I was supposed to guess who it was based on a series of questions. Except I couldn't figure out who I was (Marie Curie) and people started laughing.

"Well, they had to have known," I said dully, "because Matt's father is the assistant football coach and he wouldn't have let Matt play if he hadn't passed history."

The cops exchanged knowing glances. "What if I told you, Miss Graves," Zabriskie continued with a touch of glee, "that there wasn't a chance that Matt Houser would have been benched this season?"

Goosebumps rose on my arms. "Why?"

"Because he finished the class with a B."

That didn't make sense. "He didn't get a B. He failed."

Zabriskie reached into the folder and removed a piece of white paper with the instantly recognizable Potsdam High Panthers logo on top and, below, Matt's grades for junior year. The line for US History was highlighted in bright yellow, ending in a big, bold B.

The floor wobbled. I gripped the table edge to remain steady.

"I don't get it," I whispered, searching for a logical explanation. All those summer evenings, all that reading. Him out the door at eight sharp as if he couldn't stand one more minute. "He paid," I said. "Twenty dollars a session."

Zabriskie let out a loud, low whistle. "Wow. He must really like history to lay down two hundred bucks for no reason. Unless . . ." He paused, stroking his chin. ". . . the money was a down payment for something else. Some service you promised to provide in the near future, a way for you to apply your expertise in anatomy."

I was stunned. Had Zabriskie just implied I was an accomplice to murder?

"That's it," Mom declared, leaping out of her chair so fast it fell backward and hit the floor. "We are done. I am sick of watching you harass and intimidate my daughter, who, by the way, was only trying to do the right thing. Come on, Lily. Bob is going to hear about this."

She reached over to grab my hand when something else caught my attention. Zabriskie was dangling a ziplock bag, inside of which was the treasured Persephone necklace I'd lost last summer. Just that morning I'd been searching my dresser and under my bed for it, on the off chance it wasn't at the bottom of the quarry.

"That's Lily's," Mom said. "Where'd you get it?"

Zabriskie rose from his chair. He towered over both of us. "I'm afraid to say, ma'am, that our search team came across it on Sunday. They found it snagged on a branch in the woods on the day after Erin was murdered, not twenty feet behind her house."

NINE

The day I lost the Persephone necklace was the day Matt and I went swimming, the day he told me his secret.

We were in the middle of a record-breaking heat wave so punishing a local TV reporter cracked a raw egg on the sidewalk and filmed it frying. The sticky temperatures and lazy air were definitely not conducive to studying, especially since Matt and I could no longer go to the air-conditioned public library, not with Erin watching our every move.

Matt complained it was too humid in the usually cool cemetery to concentrate on World War I. The headstones were hotter than fireplace bricks, offering no relief from the blistering ninety-plus temperatures, and the cicadas buzzing in the woods created the aura of a Southern gothic graveyard. Some Spanish moss hanging from the trees, a glass of sweet tea, and a few drawling vampires, and we could have been on the set of *True Blood*.

I slapped a mosquito and fanned myself with a notebook. "What were the 'overt acts' that convinced Woodrow Wilson to go to war?"

Matt squinted into the bright sunlight.

"Something to do with subs?" he guessed.

"Close."

He rolled over onto his stomach. "Subs reminds me of water and water reminds me of swimming. I can't work in this heat, Graves. Let's quit this and go somewhere cool."

Couple of problems with that. For one thing, with the exam only a week away, we'd added an entire afternoon to our schedule so we could get past World War II by the end of the day. We couldn't knock off now, with the United Nations, the Great Depression, and Pearl Harbor untouched.

"But the makeup is next week," I said. "And we've barely touched the twentieth century."

"Who cares? I've crammed enough history to pass."

In light of how much money he'd forked over, his nonchalance surprised me.

"What if Erin sees us?" I said.

"Don't worry about her. She's probably lounging around her own pool with Kate and the rest of them."

I wasn't willing to risk a chance encounter, so I made another suggestion. "Sara and I have a secret spot at Miller's Creek where hardly anyone goes. We can study there."

Our hideaway was a pretty glen of soft green grass surrounded by honeysuckle bushes. With a beach bag of towels, a couple of Diet Cokes, and the latest issues of *Us* magazine, we had spent entire afternoons there reading, laughing, and wading into the babbling brook when we needed to cool off.

Matt balked. "That thing's probably a mud hole these days."

Possibly. That left only one alternative, besides the disgusting public pool: the quarry.

My mother had designated the quarry as strictly off-limits due to its unpredictable danger. Last summer, she'd been assigned the unpleasant duty of transporting a body, submerged for days, that the search-and-rescue divers had found. He was in his twenties, still wearing his gold chain, with a tattoo of an angel that, along with the rest of his skin, disintegrated upon touch.

Boo said that his body felt as slippery as leftover soap in the shower.

He wasn't the only one. Over the years, more than a dozen people had drowned in Harper's Quarry, either hitting their heads on rocks or suffering the misfortune of catching their feet in the crannies that riddled its perimeter. Most of them had been drunk. Or stoned. Often both. Stupidity was a common risk factor. As was darkness.

There were lots of myths about Harper's, like that it had no bottom and that the water reached the Earth's core, where it turned boiling hot. There were pieces of rusting construction equipment (true) and monsters (not so much) in the quarry. It was rumored that swimmers had felt their ankles tugged by invisible creatures below and that the trick was not to resist, because if you fought too hard, you'd use up all your oxygen and die. The best approach was to try to extricate yourself slowly and, most of all, not panic.

Matt eyed me cautiously. "You really want to go to the quarry?"

I shrugged. "Sure. Why not? If you know where to dive, it's okay. My aunt Boo took me once and pointed out the safe areas."

I did not elaborate that she did this after we got

the so-called "sinker" with the soap body, or that in so doing she'd faced one of my mother's extra special rants. In Aunt Boo's opinion, it was better to know how to avoid danger than to avoid dangerous places. Those were two distinct concepts people foolishly confused.

He rolled over and blinked at the sky. "I wish there were somewhere else. Erin has such a sweet setup."

Of course she did. Everything Erin had was prettier, smarter, newer, and better. "Well, I'm sorry I don't have a chichi inground pool. But if you don't want to go to the quarry, that's okay. I'll go alone." I stood and gathered my stuff.

"You can't go alone," he said, sitting up. "It's in the middle of nowhere. What if you hurt yourself? Or . . . whatever."

"Then it'll be on your conscience because you were too chicken to go."

A half hour later, Matt's truck was kicking up dust as we exited onto a dirt road that ran through a field of weeds, conquering a swath of industrialized destruction. We bounced over ruts and ditches, past discarded white fuel tanks and rusted barrels, to the broken chain-link fence. Matt boldly parked in front of a WARNING! TRESPASSERS WILL BE PROSECUTED sign that had been shot through with BBs.

My stomach knotted. Maybe this was a mistake after all.

"I thought you were cool with this," Matt said, getting out.

"I am. Just that . . ." I pointed to the sign.

"No sweat. Jacks and I have been here a million times and never gotten caught." He found the break in the fence and held it wide for me to go through.

I ducked under his arm. "To go swimming?"

"Um, no. Other stuff."

I chose not to think about what he'd been up to, or how the mustard-yellow DANGER! DEEP QUARRY! KEEP OUT! had triggered a burst of jitters in my gut. This had been my idea. Now was not the time to be a wuss.

We wound our way through the grass. Here and there were charcoal circles of extinguished fires littered with faded beer cans and melted packs of Marlboros. I dared not take off my sandals lest I step on broken glass or, God forbid, used condoms.

When we got to the edge, I let out a gasp. This was a more precarious drop than I remembered from coming here with Boo, and I wondered if she'd taken me to a different jumping-off point, since this had to be at least twenty feet straight down. The dark water below was surrounded by steep cliffs and jagged rocks striated with gashes left over from mining. Also, the slate surface was fragile. A scrape of your toe could cause it to crumble to bits.

"Piece of cake." Matt swallowed. A bead of perspiration dribbled from his temple past his jaw.

"Don't be a weenie," I bluffed, stepping out of my tan skirt and sandals. After removing my skull ring, pentagram necklace, and other jewelry, dropping them onto my skirt lying in the grass, I was practically naked aside from a black tank and underwear—bikini-style Dora the Explorer panties I'd bought for the irony. Sara had given me a raft of grief that morning when I was getting dressed after spending the night at her house.

"I'm not sure that's an area of the body Dora should be exploring," she'd said, laughing.

"At least it's not days of the week," I countered weakly, since Sara knew I had a set of those, too.

Matt didn't seem to notice, however. He just put his hands on his hips and boldly nodded in approval. "Yes, it's all going according to plan."

"Shut up. You're next."

He ripped off his shirt to reveal a pair of striped boxers peeking over the edge of his khaki shorts. I was surprised that his shoulders were so smooth, almost as if they'd been oiled.

"Do I pass?" he asked, spreading his arms wide.

My stomach flipped. "In a pinch," I said breezily. "So, who goes first?"

He reached in his pocket, threw his wallet on the ground—"Glad I remembered that!"—and found a quarter. He tossed it up and smacked it onto the back of his hand. "Heads or tails?"

"Heads."

George Washington sparkled in the sun. Great.

No going back now, I thought, inching to the edge. The dark water below was like glass. I turned to Matt.

He looked uneasy. "Don't mess up, Graves. I've got plans tonight and they don't include searching the depths of this pit for your sorry ass."

Matt gave me two thumbs up and I retreated a few paces before running outward off the edge, my adrenaline soaring.

The few short seconds it took for my feet to feel the air beneath them, to see the water rising up and then swallowing me into its shockingly frigid depths were, without question, the most exhilarating of my life. Everything around me came into sharp focus—the cliffs on the other edge, a seagull flying far from home, the click of the cicadas, the smell of the rocks baking in the sun, the dropping temperature as I fell.

I hit the water and went down, farther than I'd

expected. There was paralyzing shock as my system protested the frigid water. The quarry didn't have the benefit of light, like you get in a blue swimming pool or a sandy pond. It was as black as night down there and so cold that my calves cramped.

I remembered Boo's obvious advice: *Look up.* I looked up, and there, far above me, was a small ring of white gold. The sun. No wonder people drowned at night. You couldn't figure out where to go.

Pointing my fingers to the sky, I kicked with all my might until I broke through the surface, relieved, invigorated, and tingling with the thrill of accomplishment.

"Jump!" I shouted, gasping. "It's amazing!"

Matt peered down tentatively. I found his caution very strange, since he'd built a reputation as fearless on and off the football field. He'd once climbed to the roof of the school to put a pig there because none of the seniors dared, even though it was their prank. The dude even drove down the highway with his knees!

"Seriously. It's fine," I assured him. "It's cold when you hit the water, but it feels so good." To show him, I floated on my back.

He didn't move.

"Are you really not coming in? You're just going to leave me here alone. What if something pulls me under and . . ."

He took a running leap and was off, clutching his legs to his chest. He'll sink too far if he does a cannonball, I thought as his body met the water with a terrific splash. I bobbed in his waves and treaded madly, waiting for him to emerge, and when he didn't it was my turn to be alarmed.

"Matt!" I called. "Matt!"

I dove into the darkness, my eyes taking a second to adjust. I was a good swimmer, thanks to my mother's insistence that I learn to float before I could walk. I was only ten when I learned CPR and got my American Red Cross certificate. But in the depths of Harper's Quarry, the visibility was zero.

I surfaced and paddled around valiantly searching for any sign of life.

Finally, there was an eruption of bubbles as Matt surfaced, his arms smacking the water. "Goddammit, Graves," he swore, shaking his head. "I told you I didn't want to effing do this and you made me."

I'd never seen him so furious. I was almost frightened. "I didn't do anything wrong. I didn't *make* you come in."

"You did and you know it." He aimed for the rocks and began swimming freestyle, his arms fighting the water with too much effort.

I was about to say "Sorry" when I caught myself.

He was a big boy. If he didn't want to jump in, he didn't have to. It wasn't my fault that he'd freaked down there.

He hoisted himself onto a large rock, holding his nose. Blood cascaded down his chin.

"Are you okay?" I asked, getting out and discovering, too late, that the rocks were like fire. I had to splash water on them to be able to sit. "Because you're acting like a total ass, you know."

He said nothing as he wiped the blood off his lips and kept his eyes averted. Embarrassed, I realized. That was why he'd gotten so angry, because he'd been ashamed about losing his cool.

We sat silently, the sun warming and drying our skins. Matt's nosebleed stopped and he seemed to calm somewhat as he reclined against an indentation in the cliff.

"My bad," he said after a while. "I don't know what happened there."

I lay next to him. With a piece of slate driving into my spine, it wasn't exactly comfortable, but I didn't want to complain. "I've never seen you so pissed over nothing."

He sat up and looked away. "Remember when I told you about James, my twin brother?"

Oh, crap. "Don't tell me he drowned."

"Thanks to me."

"And that's why you don't like to swim." I sighed at my incredible insensitivity. "What happened?"

Matt plucked a weed that grew through the rocks. "We were at our cabin on Lake Wallenpaupack, an awesome place right on the water with a dock and rocks to dive off and those black inner tubes James and I loved playing in."

I watched his face, how his brow furrowed as he told the story. One Sunday morning, they'd awakened way early, as little kids do. It was mid-July and already it was hot. James wanted to go swimming, but Matt told him they couldn't go without their parents.

"But he went anyway," I guessed.

Matt nodded. "I tried to wake up Mom and Dad. I banged on their door. They had it locked and the window air-conditioning was on full blast. When I gave up to go get James, he was clinging to a tube and drifting away from shore. I wanted to save him, but I couldn't float and . . . neither could he."

"Oh God!" I had an image of Matt as a skinny shrimp, standing on the dock and calling frantically for his brother. I wanted to reach out and tell him it would be okay. I wanted to turn back the clock and shake his parents awake. I wanted to jump in that water and rescue James myself.

"I saw him go down," Matt said, his eyes tearing. "One minute, he was holding on to the tube, kicking, and then the wake from a passing boat flipped him and he was gone." He snapped his fingers. "Just like that. *Gone*."

I covered Matt's hand with mine. There was nothing to say, so we just stayed like that, him pretending not to cry, me pretending not to notice.

"I swear Mom and Dad haven't forgiven me. They say it wasn't my fault, but I know what they really think."

"What?"

"That I didn't try hard enough to stop him from going out or to wake them up. Once, Mom even asked me if I'd dared James to go on the tube, since I used to do stuff like that—bet that he wouldn't eat a worm, which he would." He grinned to himself. "He was such a great guy."

I remained silent the way Mom did whenever clients broke down in her office, unburdening their guilt and regrets to a woman they barely knew. A welcome breeze blew into the quarry. I curled my arms around my knees and let an awkward pause settle between us.

Matt scratched a stone against a rock. "Sometimes I wonder if I really did dare him and I just suppressed the memory. Maybe I'm a psychopath."

"You're not a psychopath," I said softly.

He shrugged. "I could be. Why didn't I stop him, then? Why didn't I tackle him and sit on him like I did all the time?"

"You were only five, Matt. It was an accident."

"So they say."

"Have you ever thought of going to a shrink to deal with this?"

"No shrinks. No way."

"Why?"

"Because what if I'm right? What if I'm misremembering everything that happened and I really did dare James to go? What if I really am . . . a killer?"

I refused to even entertain the possibility. "You're not, okay? Psychopaths are cold and clinical. They don't care about anyone else except themselves."

"I care about myself. A lot."

"As well as other people. Look how good you are with Erin. A million other guys would have broken up with her by now. But you stick with her because you love her."

"I'm not sure I do, still." Another pause. "I'm not sure I ever did."

"Okay, think back to that day at the library when Erin was on the steps throwing a fit. You were so sweet to her, Matt. I know because I saw you stay and talk to her."

He took a deep breath. "Only because I need to protect her. Like I didn't do with James."

I scooted next to him. He was warm and smelled vaguely of fresh water and summer sun. I gently rested my arm across his shoulders, surprised at how good it felt to touch his bare skin. And also, how perilous.

"You've got too much baggage that's dragging you down," I said, repeating Aunt Boo's favorite line. "Might want to bury it once and for all."

Matt leaned into me. "Well, you're the gravedigger here. Think you can help?"

"I've got a shovel!"

Eventually, we climbed the cliffs and reached the top, the bottoms of my feet blistered from being burned on the rocks, my fingertips raw and scraped. We got dressed and went back to his truck, driving silently to my house.

He pulled up to the curb and killed the engine. "Thanks," he said, glancing at me sidewise. "You know, I've never really told the whole story to anyone before, not even to Erin."

"Seriously? What does she think happened?"

"Just that he drowned at the lake. I never explained how I was responsible."

"You weren't—"

He held up his hand. "I know. Don't say it."

"Anyway, it was cool going to the quarry, and I'm sorry I scared you, and . . ." On impulse, I leaned over and brushed my lips against his cheek. To my surprise, he threw an arm around my shoulder and pulled me to him, nuzzling my wet hair.

"You're awesome, you know that, Graves?"

I said nothing.

"You and I are friends, right?" he said. "You won't start ignoring me in the halls when school starts up again?"

"It's you who used to ignore me."

He kissed my hair. "Not anymore. Never."

We stayed like that for a bit, and then I broke free and climbed out of the truck. Matt waited until I was inside and then peeled off. In the kitchen, I dropped my stuff on the table and went out to the back porch, where I sat down on one of our ancient marble benches and burst into tears.

Later that night, I was getting ready to take a shower when I reached into the pocket of my skirt and realized that I must have lost the Persephone necklace at the quarry. Sara and I went to look for it the next day with no luck, despite a thorough search. Either someone had taken it or it had fallen into the water, in which case, much to my dismay, it was gone for good.

Or so I thought. Until Zabriskie slid it across the table and told me it had been found at the scene of Erin's murder.

TEN

A cold drizzle was falling from a menacing gray sky when Mom dropped me off at Sara's house on the way back from police headquarters. My flimsy lie was that we had a project to do for physics.

I dashed through the raindrops up the driveway, past Sara's huge three-car garage, and down the slate path to the double French doors of their mini mansion. Aside from the professional landscaping, Sara's house was similar to every other one in the Pinewoods development, including, I assumed, Erin's. The McMartins' house had the same dramatic foyer and circular stairway, the gigantic kitchen that stepped down to a great room. Four bedrooms, four bathrooms, a formal dining room, and a backyard pool.

The one glaring exception was the absence of Halloween decorations. There were no witches or tiny white ghosts dangling from the trees. Not even a carved pumpkin. Their religion didn't allow it.

Don't ask me what religion Sara was, exactly. I'd never been entirely sure. She went to a low, white church way out in the boonies with a crazy name like First Redeemer Christ Calvary Community Chapel or something. I went once and nearly fainted when the McMartins explained that I would be there all day, but that it would be *fun* because there would be Jell-O pops and pickup basketball breaks. Also bug juice, a disgusting term for Kool-Aid.

At any rate, Sara's church considered Halloween to be a festival of Satan worship. Ditto for Christmas, which Sara's family preferred to call "Christ's birthday" and celebrated with a cake and no presents. Easter was okay as long as you left out the bunny and didn't mind being greeted with "Hallelujah! The Lord is risen indeed!" Other than that the McMartins were fairly normal, except when it came to swearing and drinking alcohol, which were also forbidden.

Or so Sara had led me to believe.

After I rang the doorbell twice and finally gave it

a good hard pounding, Sara's seven-year-old brother, Brandon, came to my rescue.

"Thanks, little dude," I said, shaking off the water. "It's wet out there."

Brandon pointed to the pentagram swinging from my neck, his eyes wide.

I swung it around so the symbol was hidden on my back. "It's okay. It's only a special type of star."

Brandon hardly talked. Speech therapists were puzzled, since his IQ tested off the charts.

I ruffled his soft fro. "You're a tiny Einstein, you know."

He smiled. That, he did. A lot.

Dr. Ken bounded into the foyer, his big feet in thick white socks. He was a large, bearded man with twinkly eyes and an easygoing personality that probably came in handy as a pediatrician. I'd never seen him even slightly peeved.

"Hey there, kiddo. Wet enough for you? Don't forget those boots."

That was another McMartin rule: no footwear in the house. Sara once explained it was a habit her parents picked up when they were missionaries in Indonesia, where poor sanitation meant deadly germs stuck to the bottom of shoes. I sat on the bench and untied my laces while Dr. Ken sent Brandon upstairs to watch a Pokémon video.

"We're trying not to let him hear what's on the news," he whispered, watching his son skip off. "What happened to Erin is too upsetting. Even for us grown-ups."

"It's on the news?" I asked, removing my left boot.

"A press conference just started." He rubbed his face with both hands. "What Carol and I can't get over is that Erin was raised the way we've tried to raise Sara and Brandon. God was at the center of her life and she was making all the right choices. And still this happened."

All the right choices. I slipped off my right boot and thought about that. It seemed wrong that teenage girls had to make all the right choices in order not to be murdered. Did that mean girls who made wrong choices were fair game?

"Let's hope they find whoever did this soon," I said.

Dr. Ken said, "Amen."

I followed Sara's father to the great room, where Sara and her mother were hunkered on the couch, riveted to the television. Perfect Bob was at a podium, flanked by Henderson, Zabriskie, and another man in a gray suit who was saying something about no suspects at this time, though he was "confident" of an arrest. So Bob had come clean with the truth. At last.

"How'd it go?" Sara whispered.

"We have to talk."

She raised an eyebrow. "Bad?"

"I need your criminal expertise."

"Shh." Carol put a finger to her lips. "They just asked if she was murdered by someone she knew."

Perfect Bob stepped forward and gripped the podium. "I can't make that speculation. However, I will say that my department is doing everything in its power to ensure that the children of our community are safe and that this will be an isolated, albeit incredibly tragic, incident."

Sara slid off the couch and we went to the foyer. "What's up?"

"I need you to drive me to Matt's house."

"Now?"

"I have to ask him about something the cops told me. In person. Come on. I'll explain in the car."

She opened the closet and got her raincoat. "I'm going to drive Lily home, okay?" she shouted.

"Be back in time for dinner," Carol called back. "Don't forget, it's Tuesday. Family night."

Sara rolled her eyes. "Everything is always family this and family that. I'm so sick of it," she grumbled, yanking open the side door to their heated garage.

There might have been disadvantages to growing up in the McMartin household—not being able to watch R-rated movies being one such example, the whole shoe paranoia being another. But there were advantages, too, like the sparkling-clean baby-blue late-model Mercedes Carol McMartin let Sara borrow without asking.

"It turns out Matt never had to be tutored in US History," I said, as we negotiated the serpentine roads of Pinewoods. "He got a B last year."

Sara gasped. "I knew something was up with that. It didn't make any sense, being able to take a so-called makeup exam three months after he flunked. Sports might rule the school, but not that much."

How had I been so naïve?

We stopped at the gate and Sara punched in the code: 110505, Brandon's birthday. It had been that for as long as I could remember.

"There's something else," I said, after the ornate wrought iron gate closed behind us. "Remember my Persephone necklace?"

Sara cranked the windshield wipers on high as we entered the main drag. "The one you lost at the quarry last summer?"

"It's not lost. It's currently in the possession of the Potsdam PD. The cops found it dangling from a branch in the woods behind Erin's house."

Sara turned to me, her shock highlighted by the

glow of traffic. "How?"

"I don't know. I can't even think."

"The murderer intentionally put it there, I bet. How sick is that?"

A blinding light crossed the dashboard. "Holy shit!" I cried, reaching over and righting the wheel, narrowly avoiding a head-on collision.

Panicked, Sara slammed on the brakes so hard the guy behind us came to a screeching halt and laid on the horn before passing us with his window down.

"Learn how to drive your daddy's car, you ditz!" he yelled.

I thought Sara was about to burst into tears, she was so shaken. "Pull off up at the McDonald's," I said, directing her with my hands to the next driveway.

She managed to glide into the parking lot and switch off the car, resting her head against the steering wheel.

"I nearly got us both killed."

"No, you didn't," I said, rubbing her back in comforting circles.

"I was just so . . ." She lifted her head. Under the light of the yellow arches there was a red indentation on her brow. "That's got to be it, Lily. It was Matt. He placed the necklace on the branch so the cops would find it and finger you."

I sank into the leather seat feeling overwhelmed.

"It couldn't have been. You don't know him like I do. He wouldn't hurt a fly."

"That's what they said about Susan Schmaltz!"

"Who was Susan Schmaltz?"

"Only one of the most notorious black widows in history. She was a nurse who ended up marrying this superwealthy old dude, only she couldn't stand him, just wanted his money. So she found this loser. Um, not that you're a loser . . ."

"Thanks." I cut to the chase. "And she got him to kill the old man."

"No! That was the thing." Sara blew aside a strand of blond hair and swiveled in her seat, the story of Susan Schmaltz having apparently distracted her from our near-death experience. "*She* killed her husband, but she made it look like her lover did by planting tons of bogus circumstantial evidence."

"How does this relate to Matt?"

"Because what if the cops decide Matt had been planning this since last summer? He calls you up with a BS excuse about needing tutoring. He makes you fall for him. He plants a seed in your mind that Erin was capable of harming herself. He might even have told her that you were working in the graveyard last Saturday so that you two would have a confrontation." Sara peered at me earnestly. "Do you see where this is leading? The detectives might be working on a theory that you went over to Erin's and, with your expertise, made a murder look like a suicide."

"Why would I do that?"

"Any number of reasons. Revenge, jealousy, maybe wanting to get in Matt's pants."

I felt myself go hot again. "Oh, come on. That is so out there. Not even the Potsdam PD is stupid enough to buy that story."

"Maybe yes, maybe no, but I bet that's what Matt wants the cops to believe. It's *Fatal Attraction* comes to Potsdam High."

My stomach had flared up again. Not enough food and too much of Sara's warped brain. "I could see someone else setting me up, but not Matt. He's not devious."

"Oh, right. I forgot. The guy who paid you two hundred bucks to study for a makeup exam he never had to take isn't devious." She made the OK sign with her thumb and forefinger. "Gotcha."

"He didn't stand to inherit millions of dollars like Susan Smith."

"Schmaltz. Yeah, but you said yourself that more than anything he wanted to be free, and that would have been impossible with Erin plotting his future every step of the way." Sara let out a dismissive snort.

I shook my head. "Nope, still doesn't fit. Whoever killed Erin had expertise, like you said. You should have seen the crime scene photos. Those cuts followed both the radial and ulnar arteries so perfectly, a surgeon couldn't have done better. Also, considering the lack of blood, I'm almost certain she was dead before she was cut. That's a lot of complicated steps for a jock like Matt to think through and pull off without a trace."

Sara stared at the rainwater running down the windshield. "What's your theory, then?"

"I keep going back to the party on the night of the murder. According to the fax I found in Mom's office, a group of girls had been over at Erin's house. Obviously, that was Kate, Allie, and Cheyenne."

"Obviously," Sara agreed. "They're inseparable."

"Kate claimed that I had scratched Erin's face Saturday. I didn't remember doing that and when I prepped her body there weren't any scratches. I even checked the photos and her skin was flawless."

"Which means?" Sara asked.

"I don't know exactly. That Kate is lying, but why? Also, after Kate, Allie, and Cheyenne left the party, the next-door neighbor walking her dog told police she saw a boy arguing with Erin in her living room."

Sara slapped the seat. "Again all evidence circles back to Matt."

"Not necessarily. What about Alex Bone?"

"That guy is way too creepy to hang out with Erin."

"Really? I saw them hug and kiss in front of the library. They looked pretty darn close to me."

"Still, Stone Bone hasn't taken a shower in a year. I heard he did acid and literally fried parts of his brain."

"Opposites do attract."

"Or, like you said, there's a bigger issue. Something more that we don't know about." She started up the car. "At least not yet."

"At least not yet," I repeated. "Though we'll find out."

Sara was extra cautious exiting the McDonald's. "If you think I'm going to let the lazy doofuses down at the Potsdam PD railroad you into a murder charge, you have another think coming."

"And Matt?" I asked, wishing she could give him an inch.

"Him I don't care about. Never have. Never will." She flashed me an apologetic grin. "I'm sorry, Lil. You might as well stop trying, 'cause it ain't going to happen."

Matt's house was a modest brick Cape on a postage-stamp yard, but it might as well have been a mobster compound surrounded by armed guards ready to blow me away.

"I can't do this," I said, gazing at the warm light

streaming from their bay window. "What if his father answers and reads me the riot act?"

"Then ask him why his son lied about the makeup exam. Lily, you deserve an explanation," Sara said, leaning over and opening the door. "If Matt can't tell the truth then you'll know he's got something to hide."

Logically, this made sense. That didn't mean I wasn't scared, especially when I summoned the courage to go to the door and a woman who must have been Mrs. Houser answered.

"May I help you?" she asked sweetly. A dishrag was over one shoulder and her graying blond hair was pulled into a ponytail. Otherwise, she was the spitting image of Matt, with his deep brown eyes and wide mouth.

"I'm sorry to disturb you at this hour." It was dinnertime, and I could smell pot roast and potatoes, probably a daily staple in the home of two football fanatics. "But I wonder if I could talk to Matt?"

Her smile flatlined. "And you are . . . ?"

"Lily Graves. I'm in his class." I felt my cred withering with each passing moment. "I tutored him last summer?"

"Hold on. I'll see if he's available," she said, closing the door slightly and leaving me to stand in the pouring rain on the concrete stoop.

Murmuring erupted on the other side of the door, a man's voice low and harsh in an exchange with Mrs. Houser's softer tones. A second later the door swung open and I was staring up the nostrils of one of the largest men I'd ever seen.

"Coach Houser?" I asked. Not one to hang around the athletic department, I couldn't discern one of these middle-aged athletic types from another. "I'm Lily Graves. I came to speak to Matt."

"I'm afraid I can't let you."

The arrogance of that statement immediately trumped my apprehension. "You can't *let* me?"

"If what my wife said is correct, you're the girl he was hanging out with this summer. Am I mistaken?"

"Your son hangs out with a lot of girls."

"Including you."

"Including me."

"Then I will politely ask you to leave my premises. My son wants nothing to do with you, and neither do my wife and I."

My hands balled into fists. It was all I could do not to kick open the door and find Matt myself. "Excuse me, but I have done nothing wrong, Coach Houser. It's your son who owes me an explanation."

He gestured toward Sara's idling car. "Please go, before I have to call the authorities."

Seriously? This dude was twice my weight and he needed to call the cops?

I stepped off the front stoop. Sara's words of advice echoed in my ears. "Then you'll have to ask the question for me."

Coach Houser filled the doorway with his block of a body and crossed his giant arms.

"Could you ask him why he paid me twenty dollars a week to tutor him for a makeup exam he never needed? Because it seems to me like that's a moronic way to blow two hundred bucks."

The door slammed shut, and I marched back into the car. Sara was in her usual position these days, eyes fixated on the rearview.

"That went well," I said, getting in.

"Told you Matt had something to hide. And the parents know it." Sara kept staring in the mirror. "Our stalker's back."

I resisted the temptation to turn around and check. "You're kidding."

"Same gray sedan with no front license plate, right around the corner."

"What are you going to do?"

"Find out who he is." She opened the door and slid out, the Mace on her keychain aimed and ready. I got out my side too, but he was too savvy, shifting immediately into reverse and doing a U-turn up the side street so we couldn't see his plates.

Sara was literally quivering in the rain. I went over to her and wrapped her in a big hug. "He's gone. No worries."

"I'm so scared, Lil. He keeps watching me. What if I'm next?"

"You won't be. We will get to the bottom of this, I swear to God."

"We'd better go," she said, wiping away her tears with her one good hand. "You know, family night."

While the McMartins were singing "Kumbaya" and playing Sorry!, or whatever it was they did on "family night," I was refilling teacups for the wake of Joanne Snyder, a ninety-year-old widow from the Balmy Oaks Home for the Aged down the street. Only twenty or so people attended, most of them friends from Balmy Oaks and various nurses' aides who generously came to pay their quiet respects. By eight it was over and I was running the sweeper over Eternity.

It would be quite a contrast to Thursday's wake for Erin. My mother had planned for more than two hundred people, and extra space for parking had to be negotiated with Riccoli and Sons next door. Boo and Oma had been busy arranging the logistics, partly because Mom had had to devote so much energy to ensuring I stayed out of jail.

That said, after the treatment I received at the Housers', I was about ready to turn state's evidence on Matt. Sara was right. Everything had been a setup leading to Erin's murder, and I had been the "pathetic" pawn, as Kate had so thoughtfully implied.

Those were my final sad thoughts as I drifted off to sleep, exhausted from a day that began with a dream about Matt and ended with the sound of him rapping on my garden window.

I bolted upright and cocked an ear, listening.

A white paper was taped outside. I opened the window and stuck my head out, but all I saw were wet leaves swirling in the wind. The paper was damp and the blue ink had run, but it was legible enough.

Sorry about what happened tonight. My dad's a dick. Will explain everything, esp. the exam, @ the Mason's @ 12 tom. night. Best not to call/text/come to the house.
I swear I didn't kill E.
Thinking of you. Stay safe.
M

ELEVEN

Halloween was traditionally a big deal in Potsdam. It started kicking into high gear right after Labor Day, when the decrepit stores downtown plastered their windows with pumpkins and witches and moonlight madness sales offering half-off decorations. By mid-September, most lawns were dotted with fake gravestones and headless bodies on folding chairs, though nothing beat the finale: the Potsdam Halloween Parade, a mile-long festival of tossed candy.

Last night, hours after the police revealed that Erin had been murdered, the town council held an emergency session and canceled the parade. The official reason was that this was done out of respect for the

Donohue family. The real reason was that parents were scared out of their wits that a killer was on the loose.

It was as if all of Potsdam had gone crazy overnight.

"This is getting out of control," Sara said, as we arrived at school to find not only a police car with flashing lights parked at the entrance to the driveway, but every satellite TV news truck in the tricounty area.

We inched past a string of news reporters interviewing parents and other students and hooked a right into the driveway. A cop in a fluorescent green vest motioned for us to stop and lower the window.

"You guys students?" he asked, leaning in to take a not-so-surreptitious peek in the back of Sara's Mercedes. "Can I see some ID?"

We fished out our student cards. "Did something happen?" I asked, handing him mine.

"Nah. The administration just wants to make sure only students and faculty are on campus today." He scanned Sara's ID and gave it back to her without comment. "If your parents are coming to pick you up, they should know they'll have to call the school so we can put them on the list."

"Because of the reporters?" Sara asked.

"Partly." He scrutinized the photo of me in heavy black eye makeup. "This you, Lily Graves?"

"Yup. I'm in my Halloween costume today."

Dark-wash skinny jeans, a bright-blue mock turtleneck, and a kicky black-and-white herringbone jacket—all from J.Crew, all purchased by my mother in a vain hope that I would someday come to the fashion Jesus.

"What are you supposed to be?"

"The scariest thing I can think of," I said. "Normal."

The Potsdam High administration did a one-eighty on Erin. The pink poster board from the day before was dwarfed by a huge banner proclaiming WE WILL ALWAYS LOVE YOU, ERIN! R.I.P. And as soon as we passed through the metal detectors, Sara and I were accosted by social workers asking if we wanted to "process."

"First-period classes will be canceled so the principal can update the student body on this turn of events," said one, handing me a pink flyer called *Coping with Grief*. "It's mandatory."

And if Erin's death had been a suicide, what then? I wanted to ask. Would the school have gone on sweeping it under the rug?

"What I don't get," Sara said as we headed to the auditorium, "is why it mattered whether she killed herself or was killed. Either way, it's disturbing."

Hooking my pack onto my shoulder, I stood at the entrance to the auditorium and scanned for seats. Not just any seats, either.

"There are two," Sara said, pointing to the back row, our preferred spot.

"How about there?" I nodded toward the front.

"Eww. That's so close. We won't be able to talk or anything."

I eyed three perfect heads in the third row. "No, but we will be able to keep an eye on the TNs."

"Why would we want to do that?" Sara asked, following me down the aisle.

"You'll see." I took the first seat, slid my backpack to the floor, and surveyed the scene. Allie, Cheyenne, and Kate were in my periphery. They owed me a huge apology for claiming I'd been responsible for Erin's suicide, but I wasn't holding my breath.

Kate caught sight of me and quickly pretended to text. Jackson too had to avert his gaze, while Cheyenne and Allie bent their heads together and whispered.

I sat back and bided my time.

The assembly was excruciating right from the get-go. Clearly, nothing in Principal Kemple's training had prepared him for the daunting task of explaining to an auditorium full of teenagers that one of them had been murdered in her own home. And not just anyone: the class star.

"I have tried to find peace over the last two days,

and frankly, students, it has eluded me," he said, reading from a prepared speech that sounded an awful lot like a eulogy. "Erin Anne Donohue, as you know, was not only a straight-A student, a champion athlete, and an active volunteer in the community, including the local hospital, where she interned this summer in the office of Dr. McMartin. She was a person of the highest moral standards."

I cut my eyes to the TNs. Kate was biting her lower lip, her chest bobbing almost imperceptibly under her sweater. I couldn't tell if she was stifling a laugh or a sob. Jackson had his arm around her and he too was sucking in his cheeks, trying to stay composed. Cheyenne was hiding her phone between her knees. Allie had turned the slightest shade of green.

"It takes great strength of character to stand up among your peers and defend your beliefs, especially when they're not 'hip' or 'cool.'" Kemple made exaggerated air quotes. "Erin did that and more. For three years in a row, she took to this stage, on the very spot where I am today, and urged all of you to say no to drugs and alcohol."

Usually, that kind of line was met with a wisecrack from the peanut gallery. In this case, the auditorium was dead silent.

Kemple mopped his brow with a white hankie.

"She lived as she preached. She even—and, yes, I know this is 'radical'—proclaimed the virtues of abstinence."

That did elicit a few snickers. I wondered how Matt, who seemed to ooze sex, had dealt with that restriction.

"So while we leave it to the police to do their jobs and arrest the person, or persons, who committed this heinous act . . . and yes, students, I have been assured an arrest is all but imminent . . ."

I kept my gaze straight ahead.

"I think the best way we can honor Erin's memory is to follow her example and make the right choices."

Again with the right choices. Get off it.

There was a slight commotion to our right. I didn't even have to look to know what happened.

"Be right back. Have to go pee," I whispered to Sara. "Look after my stuff, okay?"

Ignoring the stern gaze of my guidance counselor, I rushed up the aisle, out the door, and into the corridor, just as Allie Woo was turning the corner to the girls' room.

I waited a beat and followed her in, locking it securely. I didn't have to worry about Allie hearing. She was too busy barfing.

"Are you okay?" I asked, ripping off a brown paper towel.

Allie gripped the sides of the toilet, panting. Her hair seemed greasy and unkempt, definitely not TN style. Although, neither was being on her knees praying to the porcelain goddess.

She backed away and staggered upright. I flushed the toilet and handed her the paper towel. "Here," I said, rummaging through my bag for the tiny tube of Crest I kept for emergencies. "You'll need this."

"Thanks." She wiped her mouth and went to the sink. Underneath the unforgiving fluorescent lights, she looked sickly.

"It's a lot to take," I said, leaning against the tile wall. "I know what a good friend you were to her."

Allie smeared the toothpaste over her teeth with her index finger and spat, turning on the water to wash it down the sink. "Not that good."

"Oh, don't be so hard on yourself. Listen, I've been around enough mourners to know that everyone feels guilty in situations like this. Even I felt responsible, for a while."

"When you thought it was suicide, you mean." Allie rinsed her mouth twice.

"Yeah. And thanks for that, by the way. You made me feel *soooo* much better."

"Sorry. That wasn't my idea."

If I recalled correctly, it had been Allie who piped

up that Matt dumped Erin because of me, but I let it slide. Winning a small battle wouldn't lead to the larger victory.

Allie unzipped her backpack and got out eyeliner and mascara. "I haven't been sleeping well at all," she said, bending toward the mirror. "I think it's all the uncertainty. One minute she was alive, then it was suicide, now it's murder."

I got out my own favorite plum lip gloss and joined her. Our eye contact was brief, but crucial. She separated her lashes and then paused. "You know something, don't you? I can tell. You have mortician information."

"What's mortician information?" I asked, holding back a laugh.

She recapped the mascara. "I don't know. Don't you guys get death certificates?"

"Usually."

"Have you seen Erin's?" she asked, spinning around so we were face-to-face. "Do you know *exactly* how she died?"

"*Exactly?* I thought her wrists were cut."

Allie batted her heavy lashes, dotting her eyelids with tiny points of black. "Is that what it says on the death certificate?"

"Don't know. I figured you would."

"Why would I know?"

"Because you were there Saturday night, along with Kate and Cheyenne and"—I smacked my lips—"of all people, Alex Bone."

Allie didn't even balk. "Where did you hear that?"

Someone banged on the door. Sara shouted, "Open up. I've got all your stuff and it's heavy."

I wet my thumb and wiped toothpaste from the corner of Allie's mouth. Allie recoiled slightly.

"See you at the wake tomorrow," I said cheerfully. "I'm sure police will be crawling all over the place. Maybe they can tell you what you want to know."

Grabbing her backpack, Allie was so flustered that she couldn't even turn the lock. I had to do it for her.

"Watch it!" Sara barked as Allie smashed into her on the way out. "Geesh. Did you see how pale she was? Like she'd seen a ghost."

"Almost," I said. "Except worse."

The hours until I was to meet Matt at the Mason's tomb seemed interminable. Fortunately, there were tons of trick-or-treaters to keep me distracted, although they were visibly disappointed when I answered the door in my Halloween costume. I don't know what they were expecting—a girl in a floor-length lace gown with black lips, perhaps?

"Do you like 'em stiff?" asked a wise guy, who was way too old to be begging for candy. There was one every year.

I responded with the usual. "I don't know. Guess I'll find out when you're dead, huh?"

Then I tossed a handful of Reese's, closed the door, and headed downstairs to see what was up with Boo, since Mom was out with Perfect Bob. Halloween was a guaranteed night off in the funeral biz. No one wants to hold a wake with the doorbell ringing every two seconds.

Boo was bent over Mrs. Dubovsky, slipping flesh-colored contacts under her eyelids so they wouldn't appear sunken. Mrs. Dubovsky was the other first grade teacher, the one I didn't have at Potsdam Elementary. Age had not been kind to her, I thought, assessing her apple-dumpling physique, blue hair, and a permanent frown that Boo was valiantly attempting to prop upward.

"A little help?" Boo lowered the volume on the police scanner and nodded for me to pinch the corner of the mouth while she applied an extra-thick coating of morticians' glue. "You have any Halloween plans tonight?"

"Yeah. I'm meeting up with Matt at the cemetery."

Boo squeezed the tube so hard, drops of glue sprayed

onto Mrs. Dubovsky's nose. "Shoot!" Fetching a paper towel, she gently wiped it off before it hardened. Then she redid it with painstaking care.

"You are not going to see Matt," she said. "It's not safe. Everyone was talking about Erin's murder at the salon today, and the general consensus was that the boyfriend did it."

Ex-boyfriend. "He didn't."

"Don't be so sure. You remember Carla Remson? She used to be the school nurse, and she said sometimes football players like Matt suffer concussions that go undiagnosed and turn them violent."

I lifted my fingers. "Matt is not brain-injured, if that's your theory." The smile fell. I pinched it up again. "Anyway, I have to see him. There are a whole bunch of questions I need answered and Matt doesn't want to call or text."

"That right there is alarming." She squinted at her work, lowering the side I'd been holding so Mrs. D didn't end up mimicking a demented clown. "I've come around to your mom's view, Lil. The more distance you put between yourself and him, the better."

This was a new and disappointing development. Until now, Boo had been generally cool about Matt. "What changed your mind?"

"Can't say. Sworn to secrecy."

"To Mom?"

"Who else?"

"But—"

"No buts. An oath's an oath." Boo rubbed the excess glue from her fingers. "There. How's that?"

The smile was about one-eighth of an inch higher on the right side, thereby lending a hint of skepticism to Mrs. D's smirk, as if she were still ribbing some poor kid for missing school picture day.

"Excellent. Could not look more like real life."

I wanted to talk some more about Matt, but apparently rigor had begun and Boo needed my assistance to help arrange Mrs. D's arms into position. This was a bone-breaking job, sometimes literally, and it required all our strength to cross the forearms and arrange the elbows. By the time her hands were peacefully intertwined, my own muscles were sore.

"Pay attention," Boo said. "I'm going to show you a technique that will save your life. If some guy is attacking you—"

"Are we talking Matt here?"

"Whatever, trip him to the ground if you can, sit on him, and quickly do this." She took both her thumbs— nails painted in a zebra stripe—and pressed them on either side of Mrs. D's windpipe. "You have to do it hard and with force. No wimpy moves. Press with all your might into the carotid and jugular simultaneously, you know where those are. He'll pass out and you can get away. Now you do it."

I leaned over Mrs. D, who continued to smile peacefully as I pressed my thumbs into her wrinkled flesh. It was ridiculous.

Over the crackling police scanner, a dispatcher called for Fish and Game to pick up a dead deer by the side of Route 22. Boo shook her head. She despised that squawk box.

"Why does your mother listen to that thing?" She pulled out a scalpel and sliced into Mrs. D's neck to search for the very carotid artery I'd just been taught to cinch off.

"Because when Mom hears a ten-seventy-nine, she calls the cops personally and reminds them that she's available for transport." A 10-79 was code for coroner request. To my mother, that was like money in the bank.

After locating the artery, Boo expertly yanked it up, tugging it once or twice for slack before inserting the needle from the embalming machine. Then she did the same for the vein on the left, linking it with a tube that connected to the drain at the bottom of the stainless steel table. Since Mrs. D arrived in one piece, the transference of fluids would only be about three hours.

I was shooed out of the room for this part, since formalin, the clear base of embalming fluid, is a known carcinogen and Boo was paranoid about me getting cancer. I didn't even want to think about the latest trend of people soaking pot in the stuff and smoking it for a crazy high. If they had any idea how vile this fluid was, that it could literally rot your body from the inside out, they'd never do it.

"Could you go into my office and get the catalog on my desk?" she said, tying a blue mask around her nose and mouth. "I might as well do some inventory while I'm sitting here keeping Mrs. D company."

Boo's office was hardly more than a refurbished closet with a TV, a couple of chairs, and a desk, on top of which lay an empty can of soda and a funeral home catalog open to prep room supplies. Boo had circled in pen a set of dental simulators ("Provides a natural appearance. Flesh-colored.") and Nev-R-Lead powdered incision heal that she probably used on Erin to fuse the autopsy cuts.

I folded it closed and did a double take. Underneath the catalog, on Boo's desk calendar blotter, was a white form downloaded from the Pennsylvania Health Department's death records section to which only funeral directors and certain public officials had access.

It was a printout of the preliminary confidential

death certificate for Erin Donohue, chock-full of pertinent details.

It noted the reporting person was Mrs. Donohue. The medical examiner had estimated the time of death to be 1:00 a.m. on Sunday, October 28. The cause was still unclear: *Fatal toxicity due to unknown poisons. (Amended report to be filed.) Massive blood loss from lacerations to both wrists as secondary.*

I read that again. So my hunch had been correct. Erin hadn't died from her wounds. Those were listed as secondary causes.

But that wasn't what stopped me short. It was the two little words at the top of the next entry.

Pregnant? Yes.

TWELVE

"No. Freaking. Way." Sara's astonished voice blared from the Bluetooth system in Boo's Honda. "The girl who founded the Purity Pact was . . . *pregnant?*"

It was hard to concentrate on the road with her shouting. "I read it in black and white."

"It's like the world just flipped upside down," Sara said. "We—or at least *I*—spent an hour this morning being told by Kemple that Erin Donohue was the saint I could never hope to be and . . ."

I checked my rearview. A pair of headlights that had been with me since I pulled out of the driveway was still there. That wasn't unusual. What was unusual was that it was midnight on a Wednesday in Potsdam and hardly anyone was up and about at this hour on my quiet side of town.

Maybe I should try to lose him, I thought, taking a sudden right on Cedar Crest just to throw him off.

". . . that's it for Matt, of course. He's toast."

I went back to listening to Sara. "Why?"

"Because *obviously* he's the father. Here's the scenario: He breaks up with Erin Friday night. She tells him he can't break up with her because she's preggers and, oh yeah, being super Catholic she won't get an abortion, and just like that there goes his precious freedom so he kills her. It happens all the time."

"He might not be the father. It could be Alex Bone."

"You and Alex Bone. Give it up, Lil. Matt was dating her for years. Of course they had sex, Purity Pact or not."

I took another right on Swaymore and tried not to think about Matt having sex with Erin.

"It's a statistical fact that women are more likely to be victims of domestic homicide when they're pregnant," Sara said. "There was this episode of *Happily Never After* where this guy from Boston claimed he and his wife were carjacked on their way back from a birthing class when—"

I got to the middle of Swaymore and slowed, waiting. Two seconds later, the headlights rounded the corner.

"Sara," I cut in breathlessly, "I think I'm being tagged."

"What?"

"He's been with me since I left home. It didn't bother me until I got to Cedar Crest and noticed he was still on my tail."

"Where are you now?"

"At the intersection of Swaymore and Easton Ave."

"You know what you should do? Pull into someone's driveway and let him pass."

"What if he doesn't?" I said, peering for a driveway that looked fairly deserted.

"Then I'll call 911 on the landline. I'm right here for you. Now, do it!"

Without using my blinker, I swung right and prayed whoever lived there didn't have mean dogs. The car behind me almost stopped dead in the street, then, after a moment's hesitation, took off, squealing around the corner on two tires so loudly that a light went on in the top floor of the house.

"I heard that," Sara exclaimed. "Was that him?"

"Yeah." My hands were shaking on the wheel.

I was so nervous I could barely remember how to reverse, accidentally shifting into neutral and almost stalling in my eagerness to get out of there before the car returned or the homeowner came outside. I couldn't decide which was worse.

"That nearly gave me a heart attack," I said, breathing deeply and trying to remember how to get to Hillside Cemetery, a hangout I'd been to a thousand times. It was late and I was tired, hungry, and emotionally spent from the roller-coaster week. Adrenaline was the only thing keeping me going, and after the spike from the stalker, it was plummeting fast.

But I could not give up. Not now when the evidence against Matt looked more ominous than ever. I'd been born and raised in Potsdam and I knew how it worked in this two-bit town. Once people got an idea into their heads, they wouldn't let it go.

Which meant even if the police never charged Matt formally, he would always be suspected of murdering Erin and getting away with it. For him, scholarships might be lost. For me, it could be the future of the Ruth B. Graves Funeral Home. Reputation ruled the funeral home industry. And nothing would trash our rep faster than an allegation that I had been Matt's coconspirator.

Not to mention that the real killer would be walking free, preparing to strike again. That scared me more than anything.

"Lily?" Sara asked. "Are you still there?"

"I'm still here," I said, parking the Honda at

Tip-Top Dry Cleaners across the street from the cemetery. "Just thinking."

"I wish you'd forget this and go home," she said wistfully. "It's Halloween at midnight in a cemetery. You know how crazy people get around here."

I removed the key from the ignition and switched to my phone. "Don't worry. Matt will be waiting for me."

"Exactly."

After we hung up, I sat in the car, rubbing my sweaty palms on my jeans, trying to get my heartbeat to slow. Weapons. That was what I needed. Something I could use to defend myself, since I wasn't too sure about that move Boo had just demonstrated.

Flipping open the glove compartment, I searched past the driver's manual and insurance packet for anything handy. Tire gauge. AAA card. Flare. And then I found it: an aneurysm hook. It was about the size and weight of a light screwdriver, and the sharp angle at its metal end allowed you to puncture flesh and lift out a blood vessel.

"Bless you, Aunt Boo," I whispered, giving the tool a loving smack.

To add to Boo's awesomeness, I found a fresh can of flesh preserver wedged under the passenger seat. This car was a treasure trove of riches, I thought, deploying the spray and immediately wishing I hadn't. The fumes were so noxious, I had to open the door for oxygen.

With the aneurysm hook stuffed into the back pocket of my jeans and the can of flesh preserver in the pocket of my fleece hoodie, I dashed across the street to the graveyard, squeezing through the familiar hole in the fence. My sixth sense urged me to do as Sara said: to go home, to flee.

But all the other five told me it was too late.

I'd been spotted.

The figure behind the angel tomb near the top of the hill wasn't a ghost, though local legend had it that a spirit haunted that grave. Spirits were ethereal and white. This one was wearing a Potsdam Panthers athletic jacket, and it looked perfectly solid.

"Matt?" I hissed into the chilly darkness, my breathing heavy as I trudged up the hill, one hand on my aneurysm hook, the other on the can of flesh preserver. "Is that you?"

He disappeared.

"Matt!"

Nothing. Now the only sound was the crunching of my boots through leaves. The rose granite gravesite where we used to study was vacant, so I headed farther up toward the woods—toward our tomb. After all, that's where he said he'd be, right?

"Right," I answered out loud, to no one.

Wind rattled the bare branches over my head as a figure stepped out from behind a stone obelisk, his face an unreal white. I stopped, my heart doing a two-step when he began to trudge purposefully in my direction.

A fluttering erupted in my chest. "Don't mess, Matt."

The approaching figure said nothing, which freaked me out even more. I felt like I was the dumb blonde in a teen slasher movie, which was not a comforting thought.

From the ambient light of the city below, I could make out jeans, and he was definitely wearing a Potsdam Panthers jacket plus—oh, come on—*a white hockey mask.*

So not funny.

"Jason Vorhees?" I said. "A little eighties, don't you think?"

"I'm glad you came, Lily," he drawled. "I missed you."

Drunk or drugged, I decided, backing up, chills tingling my spine. Either way, he wasn't Matt, and it crossed my mind that maybe the note I'd found taped to my window the night before had been placed by someone else. Like the stalker who'd been following Sara and me.

"Stay back!" I ordered, holding out the spray. "Don't make me use this."

"What's wrong, baby? It's me," he slurred, stepping closer. "It's Matt."

Over his shoulder, the hazy form of someone else emerged. There were two of them. I needed to get out of here. Fast.

"Look. I don't know who you are or what you want, but this is totally creeping me out. So I'm going to go," I said, my voice trembling. "Also, my mother's waiting at the corner in a car that happens to be driven by the chief of police so, you know, there are complications."

"Yeah, right." Jason Vorhees grunted. "You're alone. I know it. You know it. Let's just admit it."

Not quite yet. The other figure had started running, fast and silent like a true panther. Soon, the rest of him came into view—the short brown hair, the Panthers jacket, open and flying behind him—and I was filled with relief. This was the sprint of the fastest in Pennsylvania high school football.

With one swift move, I gripped my aneurysm hook and drove it into Jason's eyehole. He clutched at it, swearing and flailing about, confused and alarmed—as he should have been because, hey, there was an aneurysm hook in his eye.

"Ow!" he yelled, ripping off the hook and flinging

it into the bushes. He slid a hand under his mask and covered his eye. "I'm bleeding."

"Maybe this will help," I said, spritzing him with the flesh preserver for good measure.

That was the final straw. He reeled backward, gripping his throat. "What the . . ." He coughed, pounding his chest in a futile effort to eliminate the gas.

"Lily!" Matt yelled. "I'm here."

At the sound of Matt, Jason took off, hacking and coughing down the row of tombstones with Matt on his heels. I figured there was no way Jason could outrun Matt and his legendary speed, but I forgot that most football fields weren't booby-trapped with veterans' markers, one of which unfortunately caught Matt's ankle.

He took a flying leap, arms outstretched, and landed face-first on the grass, his head narrowly missing a stone by inches.

While Jason made his escape.

I rushed to Matt and fell on my knees. "Oh my God! Are you okay?" I said, trying with all my might to roll him over.

He opened and closed his jaw like a fish and gave up, the wind knocked out of him.

"Did you leave that note on my window last night?" He nodded.

"Then who was that guy?"

He shook his head.

"Whoever he was, he knew I was meeting you. He used your name," I said, pushing Matt's jacket off his shoulders to give him air.

He pulled himself onto his elbows. "Sorry. I almost had him."

"It's okay." I squinted toward the woods where he'd disappeared. "Guy seemed pretty wasted, so he was probably a friend of yours." I tried smiling. "Where were you when I needed you?"

"Waiting in the tomb for about an hour. I went to go look for you at the bottom of the hill, thinking maybe you were too frightened to come here alone, when . . ."

"As if I've ever been anything but at home in a graveyard," I joked.

He stood and brushed himself off. I'd never realized how tall he was before. And how good he smelled. Pure, unadulterated boy.

I stood too, suddenly feeling awkward. So many things I'd wanted to say, questions to ask, and I was speechless.

"I'm sorry," he said again. "For everything. For what Erin did to you and how you've gotten roped into this. For the shitty way my dad—"

I reached over and covered his mouth to make him shut up. "Don't."

He licked my palm, like old times. Then he took my hand in his warm one, gave it a squeeze, and said, with such earnest seriousness that I quit smiling, "All I've been able to think about is you and how I'm going to get you out of this."

"We'll get out of this together," I said, squeezing him back. "But first, I need some answers."

"I thought so." He casually slung an arm over my shoulder and said, "Let's go to the Mason's tomb. I don't know about you, but I'm not really in the mood to be dealing with any more wasted trick-or-treaters."

The Mason's tomb had been Matt's brilliant find. When Erin was at her nuttiest around the beginning of August, crashing our study sessions at the library and then the graveyard, he'd found a place where we could meet virtually undetected.

It was the abandoned Hardwick family mausoleum, a squat, crumbling stone building flanked by Greek columns and empty urns. We nicknamed it the Mason's tomb because a Mason's symbol was chiseled above the heavy bronze door.

I wasn't a fan of cemetery vandalism, having grown up listening to Mom's rants about the callousness of juvenile delinquents who smashed locks and thoughtlessly destroyed stained glass windows with little regard for the deceased. But Matt hadn't been the first to break into the Mason's tomb, and he likely wouldn't be the last. Besides, it wasn't as though we'd be desecrating the graves.

Matt pushed open the tomb door and turned on a Coleman lamp. Immediately, a golden glow spread over a space not much bigger than my closet at home, except my closet wasn't made of stone and covered with cobwebs.

He closed the door, and I took my usual seat on a bedroll he kept so our asses wouldn't freeze. Being here brought back memories of last summer, when we were young and naïve and sweet.

Death ages a person, fast. Murder, even faster.

Matt plunked himself down next to me, our legs touching. "Okay, shoot. I'm ready."

"Before I say anything, I want to tell you how sorry I am about Erin. This must be awful for you."

He draped his arms on his knees and nodded. "Not half as bad as for her parents. She's their only child."

Was, I thought. "Have you seen them?"

"Been to their house every day. They want me to stand in the receiving line with them at the wake tomorrow."

That was going to be awkward. "So they don't think you . . ."

He shook his head, looking not at me but at a spot

on the floor between his knees. "I don't know if they're in denial or what. But they're treating me like the son they never had and they keep saying how I'll be part of the Donohue family forever."

Yup. Denial. "Can I ask," I said gently, "if they know about Erin's . . . *condition*?"

He snapped his head up, his brown eyes afire. "What do you mean, 'condition'?"

This was going to be harder than I'd expected. "Brace yourself, but Erin was pregnant."

His shoulders slumped. "Oh, that's what you mean. Yeah, they know."

"And you?"

"I found out on Friday. Kate called me and said I needed to get over to Erin's house because she had big news and wasn't taking it well."

My lungs tightened. "Hold on. It was *Kate* who told you?"

"You know how girls are. They tell each other everything."

Before the father? "Um, not sure I remember reading that in the handbook."

Matt looked puzzled, and then it dawned on him. "Oh, no. I know what you're thinking." Bringing his hands up defensively, he said, "It wasn't my baby."

I wanted to believe him so much. But I also was

tired of playing the fool. "Come on, Matt. You and I both know that Purity Pact crap was just to please her parents. You and Erin have been together forever. Of course you were hooking up."

He blushed to the tips of his ears. "Depends on how you define hooking up."

Now, it was my turn to blush. "Right."

"I mean we *did* stuff, just not *that*."

"Enough to keep her membership active in the Purity Pact."

"Kind of. I guess." He rolled his eyes. "The stupid Purity Pact. Her father actually gave her a diamond, like an engagement ring, for being a virgin and 'wed to him.' How sick is that?"

I assumed Matt meant that not in a good way. "So, if it wasn't your baby, then whose was it?"

"That's the question, isn't it?" he said. "When I got over my shock, I told her I was there for her, and she told me it was not my baby and therefore none of my business. I'll admit, the whole thing had me pretty messed up."

I leaned into him. "Don't take it personally. Just think what it must have been like to have been in her position. Founder of the Purity Pact gets knocked up? Reason enough right there to commit suicide."

"Except everyone assumed she killed herself because I'd broken up with her." He stood and thrust his hands in his pockets. "It just made everything so much worse. Erin's dead. I have to deal with that. Then I have to wonder if somehow I was responsible."

I said, "How badly did she take the breakup?"

"Not bad at all. There she was, pregnant by some other guy and telling me that I wasn't as mature and responsible as he was and that he was going to do the right thing. So I said, sort of angrily, 'Then I guess you don't need me.' And she said . . ."

Matt stopped.

"What? What did she say?"

"I don't want you to feel guilty."

"Please. I'm the daughter of Ruth Graves. I was born feeling guilty. What did she say?"

He sat down again. "She said, 'It's okay, because you don't need me, now that you have Lily.' I was so pissed, I just left."

"Oh." It was kind of him to omit the expletives and the word *freak*, which Erin had undoubtedly used instead of my real name. "And that was it?"

He bowed his head. "Pretty much."

"It wasn't your fault," I said, sliding an arm around the back of his neck. "James didn't die because of you, and neither did Erin."

He exhaled heavily. "I've been telling myself that, but it's not sinking in."

"You know what I think?" I said. "I think whoever killed Erin knew about you and me and her." I carefully sidestepped the term *love triangle*, since I didn't want to go there. "And they timed the crime so that the police would naturally assume you and I committed the murder."

He frowned. "A setup? That is both very weird and very disturbing."

"And very frightening."

"No shit. If you get charged for this, I will never forgive myself. It just doubles the pain."

"We will not let that happen." I removed my arm and hopped up, my mind churning. "Let's start with the facts. Where were you on Saturday night?"

"In my room, on my bed, staring at my ceiling, feeling shitty about Erin."

"That's healthy. Any witnesses?"

He shook his head. "The cops are all over that."

Of course they were. "Next question. Who do you think is the father?"

Matt said, "No clue."

"Really? How about Alex Bone?"

"That wimp?" Matt scoffed. "Erin told me about him. All they did was talk about writing and poetry. That day we saw them at the library, he gave her a book of poems by some dude named Ginsberg. I read a few.

They sucked."

"He's a little alternative."

"So's Stone Bone. He's such a loser, working at the coffee shop, living at home with his mom. I mean, the guy's in his twenties. Be a man."

"Some girls get tremendous pleasure from turning frogs into princes."

"That's Erin. She was always pushing me to dress better and take harder classes. That's how I ended up in US History, because she said I should challenge myself."

That explained a lot. I started pacing and counting my steps . . . one . . . two . . . three. That was all the length of the tomb would allow. "Okay, so the first thing we have to do is find out what Alex Bone was up to on Saturday night. I have reason to believe he was at a pity party Kate threw for Erin."

Matt raised an eyebrow. "How did you hear about that?"

"I have my sources. Secondly, we have to find out what they were doing at the party."

"Doing?"

"Drugs. Alcohol. According to the preliminary death certificate I just saw, the cops are running toxicology tests, and they don't do that unless they have probable cause."

He looked utterly stunned. "It's like she was two different people. The good Erin and the bad Erin. I'm looking back on our three years together and asking which part of her was real and which part of her was a lie."

That rang a bell. I quit pacing and crossed my arms. "Speaking of which, do you mind telling me why you lied about failing US History and why you spent two hundred dollars being tutored for a test you didn't have to take?"

"Don't get mad."

"Why would I get mad? I made two hundred bucks."

"I did it because . . ." Matt rose and came close, which put me at a distinct disadvantage, rhetorically. It was much harder to win points against someone whose tanned abs I cherished as a precious memory. ". . . because I wanted to get to know you, and I was too stupid to think of any other way."

Surprised and secretly pleased by his answer, I played with a strand of hair that had been tickling my neck. "You could have just called. Or faked your death. It worked for Romeo and Juliet. Oh . . . wait. Scratch that."

He cracked a smile. "See, it's that kind of twisted humor that makes me . . ."

"What?"

He cupped my cheek. "Analyze Troy Polamalu's defense. Because if I don't think about football, I will go crazy thinking about you."

I felt a tingling sensation on my ass. It took a second for me to realize that it wasn't the effect of Matt about to make a pass, but my phone.

"Hold on," I said, wiggling it out of my jeans pocket. "It's probably Sara wanting to know if you've killed me yet."

He groaned.

The screen said *Barb Graves*, aka Aunt Boo. "No, it's my aunt wanting to know if you've killed me." I pressed Answer. "I swear I'll be home soon."

She did not sound happy. "You better be, because according to the scanner the police are swarming the cemetery. Apparently, someone reported that they heard a girl screaming, and I just prayed to God it wasn't you."

Had I screamed? "Okay. Well, don't worry. I'm turning the corner to Cedar Crest."

"Hurry. Before your mother gets back—and another thing: don't talk on the phone and drive."

I hung up and bit my lower lip, trying to figure out how I was going to get out of this one.

"You're not on Cedar Crest," Matt said. "What's going on?"

"The cops are here. They heard a girl scream. Boo thought it was me."

"With me, right?" Matt ran a hand through his hair. "If they find the two of us together, it will not be cool."

"Ditto. What are we going to do?"

"Classic football strategy. I head toward them and cause a distraction while you slip out the back and go through the fence to Hennessy. Where are you parked?"

"Dry cleaners across the street. Is that really a football play?"

"Kind of. When are we going to see each other again?"

"At the wake."

He nodded. "I'll find out about the party."

"I'll find out about Alex."

"Sounds like a plan." He hesitated as if he wanted to say something else. "Lil, we're going to get through this. We'll figure out who killed Erin and put this behind us."

I bent over and turned off the light so it was pitch-black. "Matt?"

"Yeah?"

"What did you do with my Persephone necklace?"

"Huh?"

"The cameo I used to wear. The goddess of death."

"That thing? Nothing. Why?"

There was the crackling sound of police radios squawking in the distance. The cops were here. "Forget it. You'd better go."

"Good luck," he whispered.

I felt something warm and vaguely rough on my cheek as he leaned down and, missing my lips, ended up brushing his lips against my ear. Then he yanked open the door and ran, hollering with all his might, while I headed silently in the opposite direction, my heart pounding for a zillion different reasons.

THIRTEEN

It is a truth universally acknowledged that *Homo sapiens* flourished because he, better than all other creatures on the planet, was uniquely hardwired to adapt. This ability to easily adjust to one's environment meant that we could learn to walk upright, create tools, and eventually even get used to the metal detector at the door in high school every morning.

But there was a downside to evolution too. The confidence I felt in the tomb was gone by morning. When I woke, I lay in bed contemplating the evidence stacked against us, and how bleak our chances were of finding Erin's killer.

"Justice is not only blind, it can be deaf and dumb,"

Sara said as we ate lunch outside in the courtyard, despite the bleak November sky that added to the general atmosphere of hopelessness. "The best homicide prosecutors are the ones who make the mental effort to put themselves in the minds and bodies of the murderers. Therefore, if you're going to abandon my advice and investigate Stone Bone instead of Matt, then the questions you need to ask are not only how Alex drugged and killed Erin, but why."

"Because she was pregnant," I said, biting into my apple with a definitive crunch.

"So? What does Alex care? When you've got nothing, you've got nothing left to lose. For all we know, a baby could have brought purpose to his otherwise nihilistic, coffee-brewing existence."

I thought of this, swinging my legs and watching the TNs cross the grass to their next classes. Kate and Cheyenne were acting as if nothing had changed, laughing and texting as they walked. Allie, however, was like a silent shadow three paces behind.

"She knows something," I said.

Sara watched her for a bit. "What?"

"That's what we have to find out."

Sara tossed her empty bottle into the recycling bin, wiped her mouth, and brought out her math notebook, flipping to a fresh page and handing it to me. "Ready?"

she asked, as a damp breeze blew back her long, white-blond hair.

During the drive to school this morning, Sara and I had agreed that any investigation we conducted needed to be cloaked in utmost secrecy. We could not risk creating a digital trail with texts or emails. Not even phone calls. Every note had to be on paper. And that paper would eventually be burned since, as every mortician knew, ashes tell no tales.

"We have to start from ground zero," I said. "We need to go to the crime scene and interview witnesses."

"Like Erin's neighbors." Sara wrote that down. "They've already been interviewed. Cops were in and out of Pinewoods for two straight days. People started to complain."

"Too bad. We have to find the next-door neighbors with the dog who saw Erin fighting with Alex."

"*Allegedly*," Sara said. "That's the Krezkys. Mrs. Krezky is super nosy. Figures she peeped in Erin's window. I sold Thin Mints to that woman for three years, and she would sit me at the kitchen table and grill me about the teachers at Potsdam Elementary."

"What are the chances that the Krezkys'll be at the wake tonight?"

"Pretty good. But let me talk to her. Not you. It's a more efficacious approach."

I looked up, slightly offended. "Why?"

"You know how some people treat those with physical disabilities like they're retarded?"

"No." Despite her obsession with Investigation Discovery, Sara was second in our class—right behind Erin. Smart was her middle name.

"Well, they do, and Mrs. Krezky falls into that category. I'd take her cold, hard cookie cash and make perfect change, and she'd speak really slowly and pat me on the head."

"You're kidding, right?"

"Am I laughing? Anyway, this is one case where I can see her stupidity working to our advantage. So let me do the questioning tonight while you're busy refilling the coffee or whatever it is morticians' kids do at wakes."

"Empty garbage," I said, writing *S* next to *Krezkys*. "In the meantime, what are you doing eighth period?"

"Cramming for the physics test during my free period. Why?"

"Because I was thinking maybe we should be doing our studying at the café."

As far as coffee shops went, the Pots & Cups—a name that was supposed to be some sort of play on the word Potsdam—fell short on the necessary inspirational atmosphere found at, say, any given Starbucks.

The concrete floor that was supposed to be hip ended up costing the establishment untold dollars in broken ceramic cups. The cappuccino maker was forever getting clogged and exploding onto the brown walls. And the jazz was just plain annoying.

At 2:00 p.m., not much seemed to be happening. Sara and I strolled in and noted with disappointment that Alex Bone did not appear to be on duty. There was only one person working, a girl, and she had her back to us.

"Excuse me," Sara said after we'd waited a good five minutes for her to finish whatever she was doing.

"Just a minute," the girl said, smearing her fingers on her apron as she came to the cash register.

I did a double take. "Tam?" I barely recognized her from last spring when she graduated. She must have gotten fifty pounds lighter since Jackson held up her soda and made fun of her for washing down a Magic Bar with a Diet Coke.

Tam smiled wide. "Hey, Lily and Sara. What are you guys doing here? I thought you were still in school."

"We are," Sara said. "Just skipping eighth period."

"Ah, yes, the pleasures of senior year," she said, her dark eyes flashing. "Wait till second semester.

You'll never go to class. So, what do you guys want? You should definitely try the pumpkin hot chocolate. Sounds gross, but . . ." She licked her lips. "To die for."

I checked to see if Alex was around. "Actually, we came here looking for someone. Alex Bone."

Tam's face fell. "Oh, him. Really? What for?"

Sara leaned over the counter. "It has to do with Erin Donohue."

"Isn't that awful?" Tam asked. "That's all anyone here's been able to talk about since the cops said it was a murder. You should have been here for the morning rush. There were people crying."

"Including Alex?" I asked.

Tam bent back and looked out the window toward the patio. "You see him out there?"

She pointed to a set of tables under the awning that faced the alley. Sure enough, there sat Alex Bone holding a lit cigarette between his fingers as he scribbled something in a journal. Now that he was up close, I was shocked at how old he seemed, with long, stringy black hair pulled into a ponytail and a soul patch under his lower lip.

"Is he supposed to be working?" Sara asked.

"He's on break, though he claims he's too depressed to deal with the public, so the manager has him cleaning equipment," Tam said. "But all he's done since

Erin died is sit and write and smoke and drink coffee while the rest of us pick up his slack. I want to kill him myself."

Sara read my mind. "Can we get two pumpkin hot chocolates?"

"Sure, I'll bring them out to you," Tam said.

At the glass door to the patio, Sara stopped me. "Look, I don't think we should mention the pregnancy unless Stone Bone brings it up."

That struck me as odd, since that was one of our main reasons for talking to Alex. "Why?"

"Because it's not cool to spread personal information that you got from a confidential death certificate. I'm surprised you're not more worried about the legal ramifications, Lil. You could get in serious trouble."

Sara was right. She usually was whenever it came to legal stuff. "I guess finding a murderer is more important than obeying the law."

She pushed open the door, clearly dismayed by my lack of respect for bureaucratic protocol.

The temperature must have dropped ten degrees while we were in the café. The long sleeves of my knit dress felt flimsy in a breeze that was almost wintry in its sharpness. Sara found a small wrought iron table in the corner and rubbed her good hand over her bad arm, though she had on a warm baby-blue cashmere turtleneck.

"Feels like it's going to snow," she said loudly, to attract Alex's attention. "Wish I had your coat."

Alex did not look up from his writing or offer his coat, which was draped artistically over his shoulders. We brushed dead leaves off our chairs and positioned ourselves so that I had a good view of him while appearing to watch the foot traffic parading on the cross street. He scribbled madly, occasionally crossing out words with violent strokes, pausing now and then to sip his coffee or puff on his cigarette.

"Cough, cough!" Sara made a big production of faking an asthma attack. "Can you believe people still smoke in this day and age?" She waved her hand back and forth. "Cancer much?"

Alex calmly placed his pen on the notebook and rotated in his chair. "It's a free country. If you don't like it, may I suggest you find somewhere else to sit?" He trailed his fingers toward the door. "Perhaps inside, from whence my kind has been banished."

Tam appeared with our pumpkin hot chocolates and, sensing the tension, cautioned Alex with a scolding glare. "Now, now, Al," she said, placing our cups on the table. "Let's play nice with Sara and Lily."

He must not have seen me before because as soon as Tam said my name, he got all excited, as if we were long, lost friends. "Lily Graves? Hey, how are you?"

"Um, hi, Alex." I smiled as Sara stifled a laugh with a gulp of hot chocolate.

His eyes were so red, they almost glowed. "You know, when I was at that pit called Potsdam High, you were the only one I thought might be able to understand my interests, seeing as how you too were mocked and ridiculed for yearning to be among the dead."

I shifted uncomfortably in my chair. "I don't know if I *yearned* to be among the dead, exactly. Since I live in a funeral home, the dead pretty much come with the territory."

Sara put down her cup. "You love the dead!" She cut her eyes to Alex, a cue to play along.

"Oh, the *dead*. Yes, I suppose that's why I'm having such a hard time dealing with Erin Donohue's murder, because I know—as do you, I'm sure, Alex—how death is so . . . permanent."

"What a segue." Sara kicked me under the table so hard I nearly yelped.

Alex stubbed out his cigarette. "It's especially hard for me, because not many people are aware of this, but Erin and I were *very* close."

"Really?" Sara said, resting her cheeks on two fingers. "How close?"

I kicked her back. She blinked, but otherwise acted as if she were hanging on his every word.

"So close that . . ." He shook out a cigarette from his pack and lit it with a pink Bic. Then he exhaled and went on. ". . . I think I know who killed her."

"You do?" I said. "Wow."

Alex played with the silver lip ring at the corner of his mouth, debating, I supposed, whether to divulge this nugget of info. "I must explain my relationship with Erin." He took another drag. "She used to come into the café every morning in her prissy clothes with not a hair out of place and ask for a chai soy latte, no sugar. Just another Potsdam homecoming queen wannabe, right?"

I said, "Sara and I call them the Tragically Normals."

He extended his cigarette. "Tragically Normal. I like that. Anyway, one day she came in clutching a volume of Emily Dickinson, and when I handed her the usual chai soy latte, no sugar, I said, 'Oh. I could not stop for Death, so Death kindly stopped for me.'"

I dared not look at Sara for fear of cracking up.

"That started a conversation about poetry, and the next thing I knew, we were out here at this very table . . ." He gestured casually to where he'd been sitting. ". . . talking about poetry and books as if we'd just learned how to really breathe."

Sara raised a questioning eyebrow. "Even with all that smoking?"

Alex clasped his hands to his chest. "You have no idea how refreshing it was to meet a true fellow intellectual. There was just one obstacle. While I had managed to free myself from most institutions, Erin was still very much confined."

"What do you mean by 'institutions'?" I asked. "Like prison?"

Sara was going to kick me for that, too, but I blocked her with my foot.

"Actually, I have done some time behind bars," Alex said with a bow. "However, I'm referring to the other institutions that drain our creativity—school, church, family."

"I hear that!" Sara said, raising her hand. "School, church, family. Welcome to my prisons."

"See?" Alex said. "For Erin, too. There was so much pressure on that girl to compensate for other people's failings by being the best at everything." He ticked off on his long, spidery fingers: "The best at academics. At athletics. At volunteering. Along with being the best daughter, girlfriend, and, though this is an oxymoron in my opinion, she was even the perfect virgin."

Alex may have been a skeeve, but he was raising interesting points. I'd honestly never stopped to consider the pressure Erin had been under or how she dealt with all those expectations of perfection.

"So how did you help?" Sara asked.

"I gave her permission to break her bonds. I told her she didn't have to be her parents' puppet, that rules were meant to be broken early and often." Then he leaned close and whispered, "And I got her a little weed."

The dude wasn't called Stone Bone for nothing.

Sara leaned back, hiding her bad arm under her good one. "How did Erin take it?"

"Like a fish to water."

The door opened again, and this time Tam was more than curious about Alex. She was downright pissed. "You were supposed to be back on duty ten minutes ago. You're not the only one who needs a break, you know."

Alex ground his cigarette under the heel of his boot and got up from his chair, swinging the duster like a matador with a cape. "Been nice chatting with you ladies," he said, closing his notebook. "Next time you stop in, the coffee's on me."

Tam untied her green apron and handed it to him. "Here. It's the only clean one left."

"Wait," I said, just remembering. "You never told us who you think killed Erin."

He pulled his head through the loop of the apron. "Think about it. Who was on her case? Who was mad that she was experimenting with freedom? Who found her body?" He shrugged. "Obviously, it was her parents."

"Whoa," Sara said, when he'd gone. "Talk about intense."

Tam took his seat and elbowed his cup aside. "Alex isn't that intense, just stoned twenty-four-seven. He's like one of those guys from the antidrug commercials. Lots of big talk and no action. Look. He's supposed to bus the tables and he leaves his own cup."

She was about to pick it up when I practically leaped from my chair and threw myself onto the table. "Do you mind?" I said. "I'll pay you for the cup, but I'd like to take it with me."

Tam made a face. "Why?"

"It's complicated, but I have my reasons."

After we gave Tam a tenner for the cup, I slipped a napkin under the handle and dumped the contents in a planter, putting the cup securely in my bag. Sara and I left the patio and went back to her car without detouring through the café.

"So," Sara said, as we drove off. "Do you think Alex is the baby daddy?"

"Absolutely not," I said. "Any guy who notices if a

girl's clothes are prissy or if she has a hair out of place isn't interested in the opposite sex."

"Then they were just friends like he said."

"Or something else." I checked my bag to make sure the cup was in one piece. "At any rate, we'll find out soon just how close they really were."

FOURTEEN

Mom was in such a tizzy when I got home that she didn't even notice I was late.

Snow was forecast. Not a lot, just a few flurries, but enough of a nuisance that if the line for Erin's wake stretched from our front door to the outside, as we expected, people would be griping about how Riccoli and Sons had done a much better job of handling the mayor's calling hours last year.

I hid my bag in the locked hall closet so I'd have it at the ready if I got a moment alone with Perfect Bob. In the three years Mom and Bob had been dating, I couldn't think of a time I'd ever wanted to get him alone. But now there was no one I wanted to speak to more.

Besides Matt.

"There's no use in worrying about the weather," Oma said soothingly as my mother anxiously watched our retrieval guy, Manny, tack an awning above our walkway. "We'll get a few space heaters, some blankets, and I'll make hot chocolate."

"Sounds more like a tailgate party than a wake," chimed in Boo, who was at the kitchen table, high heels on the chair, folding pale-lavender memorial cards. "I say let them suffer. A teenager was murdered, for Chrissake. No one's going to grumble about a little snow when you've got two devastated parents barely able to stand."

Boo was right. When tragedy struck, people wanted to suffer—as long as they didn't have to suffer *too* much.

"I'm with Auntie on this one," I said, inspecting one of the memorial cards. It featured a photo of Erin smiling in her prom dress. Below, her name appeared in raised silver print.

ERIN ANNE DONOHUE
MAY 1, 1995–OCTOBER 28, 2012
A LIFE THAT TOUCHES OTHERS GOES ON
FOREVER . . .

It especially goes on forever when that life touches you with sharpened stiletto nails, I thought, massaging my itchy scars.

Mom turned away from the window and, as if just noticing I'd arrived, said, "Did you get the folding chairs out of storage and set them up?"

"Not yet."

"Get on it, then. We need fifty in both Paradise and Eternity. Check to make sure the displays Kate Kline and Allie Woo set up are in the right places. Is that what you're wearing tonight?"

How did she do that? Nag without stopping to breathe.

"I look fine," I said, crossing my arms over my chest.

"No, you don't. You look inappropriate."

"*Ruuuuuth,*" Boo cautioned, keeping her focus on the memorial cards. "Let it go. Lily is meeting you halfway."

Seriously. Compared to Boo or even my regular wardrobe, I was fairly conservative. No corsets or ominous heavy crosses. Just a plain scoop-neck gray sweater—tight-fitting, sure, but what wasn't in my wardrobe?—and a ruffled black lace skirt. I'd even toned down the eyeliner so it was less Sharpie, more Bic fine point.

Mom straightened her posture. "With all due respect, Barbara, I know how to raise my daughter and run this business. The Donohues are going through hell, and the last thing they need is my child directing all the attention to herself."

I was so not directing attention to myself.

Boo eyed Mom knowingly. "The Donohues are in a blur of grief. They'll never remember what Lily wears. You're just worried about what the cops will think."

I said, "You mean Perfect Bob."

"No," Boo said, tidying the stack of memorial cards. "I mean cops. After the wake tonight, the place is going to be . . ."

"Ahem." Mom cut her off. "We'll discuss that later."

Behind her, Boo pantomimed a slice through her throat.

I decided to get those chairs.

The Eternity parlor was our biggest room. It connected to Serenity via a field of dirt-defying speckled beige carpet, which led to the more secluded Paradise. Paradise was smaller, with only one bay window shielded by the frilly dove-white satin curtains found in every mortician's catalog. It smelled permanently of lemon Pledge.

This was where the family would stand, tissues

wadded in hands, to nod in polite gratitude while mourner after mourner somberly recounted some bittersweet story from Erin's past—how she once babysat their kids and taught them how to weave God's eyes with Popsicle sticks, how she always wore a sweet smile and was so pretty, so very pretty. And bright, too!

Students, friends, and awkward teenagers of whom their daughter had never spoken would claim to have had a close personal bond. If I were in the receiving line, I would wonder which of the hands I shook had killed Erin.

Call it a hunch, a sixth sense from having spent my life in a funeral home, but I knew the killer would be here. Because he knew that if he didn't show, that in itself would appear suspicious.

After setting up the chairs in Eternity and Paradise, I was lugging some more into Serenity when I almost stumbled upon the mahogany casket and froze.

It was closed, but that didn't matter. What mattered was that the last time Erin and I were alone was Saturday in the graveyard when we had our fight. I couldn't help but feel that there was unfinished business between us and that somehow she had managed to wreak more revenge on me while she was dead than when she was alive.

Okay, no, I told myself, arranging the chairs. Boo

might have claimed she "sensed" the spirits of the dead when she worked late at night down in the prep room, but I'd never had that experience, and if I did, I would pack up and move to Sara's.

Flipping on the lights, I cranked the dimmers to full brightness so I could see what Allie and Kate had tacked to the easel they'd set up for Erin. There was a framed baby photo of Erin in the bath, bubbles on her head shaped into a crown. In a white dress and veil for her first communion. As a Girl Scout selling cookies. On a nearby table, they placed one of her championship trophies, her medal as a member of Model UN last spring in Harrisburg, and a sepia-toned Instagram picture of Matt and her at the junior prom. Erin was in a skimpy pink dress, Matt gazing at her with absolute adoration.

I was thinking Allie and Kate did a lovely job when the hairs on the back of my neck rose. Slowly, I repositioned the photo of Matt and Erin and turned.

His wire frames glinted under the light as he approached the table, our ancient floorboards squeaking with each of his footsteps. Detective Zabriskie from the Pennsylvania State Police, Homicide Division, at my service.

"Lovely couple," he said, picking up the prom photo for a closer look. "Her mother tells me they were going to get married someday." Putting it down, he stressed, "*Were.*"

There was so much he didn't know, it would be laughable—if Matt's innocence weren't at stake.

"Calling hours aren't until seven," I said, setting a vase of white lilies nearby so the flowers bent gracefully.

"Guess I'm early, then." He positioned the photo next to Erin's favorite doll from her childhood, a worn teddy bear in a plaid skirt. "Heartbreaking, isn't it? Just the other day she was a baby, the apple of her parents' eyes." He ran his fingers over her baptismal gown, white with a lace bonnet. "And then some selfish bastard decides it's within his right to take her life just because she got in the way of what he wanted."

I batted my eyes, amazed that a man with his training could be so daft. "Can I help you, Detective Zabriskie?" I asked, flicking off a dead leaf that had fallen from one of the flower arrangements. "Because if not, I have some homework to do before the wake."

He strolled over to the casket and, without so much as a by-your-leave, lifted the lid. Erin was there, just as we'd left her on Monday night, eyes closed and sleeping blissfully. If Zabriskie was gambling that the sight

of her would be a shock, he was mistaken. I'd probably seen more corpses in my seventeen years than he'd
seen in his lifetime.

"We received a tip that you and Matt Houser were
in the cemetery last night."

"Oh?" Where did he get that?

"You mind telling me what you two were up to?"
he asked, swiveling away from Erin.

"Detective Zabriskie," I replied calmly. "I'm not
a cop, and I don't want to tell you how to do your
job, but you're wasting your time on Matt and me.
We didn't kill Erin. I didn't kill Erin. Matt didn't kill
Erin. Whoever did is laughing himself silly that you're
focusing on us when you should be focusing on him."

The corner of Zabriskie's mouth twisted. "Then I'll
take that as a yes, you *do* mind telling me what you
were up to."

Forget it. I couldn't win. "How about a compromise? I'll give you some info if you give me some info."

Zabriskie squinted. "Depending on the intelli-
gence, it's a deal."

"Okay. Stay right there." I went around the corner
and down the hall to the coat closet, opening it with
a key we kept under the vase on a side table. I passed
through the kitchen to get a ziplock bag, ignoring my
mother's hysterical shrieks about whether I'd set up

the stupid chairs, and returned to Serenity.

"Here," I said, slipping a pen under the handle of the cup and transferring it to the ziplock bag. "Compare the prints on this to the prints you found at Erin's house. I think you'll find it interesting."

Zabriskie pinched the bag at one corner. "What is this?"

"A cup that was used earlier today by one Alex Bone, aka Stone Bone. He's a barista at Pots and Cups and a 'friend'"—I put friend in air quotes—"of Erin's. He is also one weird dude."

"I'm sorry to disappoint you, Miss Graves, but Mr. Bone has an alibi for that night."

"What?" I said. "His mother?"

Zabriskie reddened slightly. "Well, yes."

"Now, my turn," I said. "Who called in with the tip that Matt and I were in the cemetery?"

"She didn't give her name, but I'll tell you this. She sounded young, I put her at your age, and the call was placed from a courtesy phone at the Potsdam Regional Medical Center. Have any idea who it could be?"

Immediately I thought of the Tragically Normals. They were the only ones who would have been evil enough to phone police headquarters with that kind of rumor, anything to deflect attention from themselves.

"No," I lied. "Not a clue."

Zabriskie adjusted his steel-frame glasses. "Really?"

"Really."

"That's a pity, then. Because whoever she was, Miss Graves, she is no friend of yours."

And with that, he walked into Paradise, taking Alex's coffee cup with him.

FIFTEEN

There were more mourners at Erin's wake than I could ever remember packing in the Ruth B. Graves Funeral Home. They came in vans and station wagons, spilling out in somber heaps of dark coats. Buses of field hockey players rolled in from other districts, the girls dressed in their plaid-skirted uniforms and wearing lavender ribbons in honor of the slain state champ. The entire congregation of St. Anne's Church was there, and also kids Erin went to summer camp with in the Poconos. Manny's awning didn't begin to cover the line that stretched down our long driveway to the street. In the snow.

There were also, much to our dismay, news crews.

Two news vans with their space-alien satellite dishes parked right by our gates as their reporters interviewed our guests about whether they could sleep at night knowing a "child murderer" was on the loose. In our driveway, a spotlight illuminated Channel Three anchor Brittney Freeman as she delivered a live report in the cold, dark night.

"Brittney's a lot smaller in real life," Oma said, peering through her binoculars. "I hope they get the name of the funeral home in there. This could be good for business."

"Oma! That's no way to talk," my mother scolded as she bustled into the kitchen carrying a tray of dirty coffee cups.

My grandmother shrugged and kept on spying. Mom deposited the tray by the sink, where Manny, sleeves rolled, was up to his elbows in dishwater. Then she blew back an invisible strand of stray hair and twirled toward me at the counter, setting up yet another coffee urn.

"When you're finished with that, Lily, take a stack of clean plates into Serenity and tidy up." This was followed by a mumble concerning slovenliness and human beings. "Also, Boo says the powder rooms are nearly out of toilet paper and the soap dispensers should be checked, but I don't know how you're going to get in there they're so crowded already."

She left in a whirlwind, and Boo arrived with another set of dirty dishes, much to Manny's consternation. "Has your sister-in-law not ever heard of paper plates?" he complained in his thick Puerto Rican accent. "Here am I doing everything. Hanging awnings. Directing traffic. Shooing riffraff off the lawns. Now dishes. You know, I'm just a driver, man. A retrieval guy."

"One word, lover boy," Boo said, handing me the freshly cleaned set of plates, still piping hot from the dishwasher. "Overtime. Lily, how about distributing some more memorial cards? We're running low."

"Love to." I was leaning over the table to get a fresh stack when a haunting wail pierced the hushed murmuring. The cry was something otherworldly, wild and raw.

It was Erin's mother.

Boo closed her eyes in prayer. Manny quit clattering the dishes to cross himself. No way did Elaine Donohue kill her own flesh and blood, I thought, pissed at Alex for suggesting such a thing.

"That poor woman," Boo said.

I wondered how Matt could stand next to Mrs. Donohue while she howled for her beloved daughter. I'd overheard the Donohues introducing him as "Erin's boyfriend," when he really wasn't. It had to be brutal.

"Hey, Lily. What a showing, huh?" Kate Kline was playing nice because she was on my turf.

I handed her a memorial card. Allie Woo averted her eyes and gazed at her shoes.

"TV news is here," I said stupidly. "Gotta go. Can't stop!" Frankly, this was one situation where I was glad to be working.

Sara broke away from Erin's neighbor, Mrs. Krezky, a portly woman with a simpering smile. "Be careful, dear," I heard Mrs. Krezky say. "You don't want to ruin your pretty dress."

"Whatever that means," Sara said under her breath.

I handed her half the memorial cards to make it look like she was helping. "What did she say about Saturday night?" I asked.

"You're not going to like it, Lil," Sara said, giving a card to a kid too young to read. "The guy Mrs. Krezky saw arguing with Erin that night sounds exactly like Matt. Short brown hair, Potsdam Panthers jacket, and everything."

"Those Panthers jackets are everywhere," I said, trying not to show my disappointment. I'd so wanted Mrs. Krezky to say the guy had a long, stringy ponytail. "Don't forget, the moron playing the Halloween prank had a Panthers jacket on too. Did she say what car he drove?"

"Noooo," Sara said, mindlessly handing a memorial card to an old man in line who already had one. "Then again, I didn't ask."

I led the way to Paradise. "Because I've been thinking about Henderson's police memo, the one faxed to Mom. It said the girls left in a Jeep-like vehicle, but it didn't mention another car. And since Erin's Mini Cooper was in the garage . . ."

"A Jeep?" Sara said. "That's Kate's."

"More proof that the Tragically Normals were among the last to see Erin alive," I said.

A hissing in my ear nearly knocked me off my feet. Mom. "This is not the time to socialize," she whispered. "Serenity is out of plates." But to Sara she said, "Hello, there. Aren't you ever the picture of loveliness? Thanks for helping out. You're so sweet."

Given the chance, I was sure Mom would trade me for Sara in a nanosecond.

"We'll talk later," Sara said, her finger waving bye-bye.

I went back to the kitchen, got another set of plates from Manny, and threaded my way through the throng crowding Serenity, briefly stealing a glance at Mrs. Donohue. She was smaller than I remembered, and old. Her normally strawberry-blond hair was gray at the roots, and tears rolled down her cheeks. Matt, tall and strong, kept an arm around her shoulders while her husband teetered, looking dazed.

I gave Matt a thumbs-up. He returned a sad smile.

"Is this decaf?" Detective Henderson had his hand on the urn. "Because this is my third cup and if I have any more caffeine I won't sleep until Sunday."

"That's your fifth cup," I said, depositing the plates. "You must be bouncing off the walls."

"All part of the job." He held out his cup and pressed the lever. We both watched the coffee pour like this was the most fascinating experiment ever. Henderson sniffed at the carafe of cream and added a slug to his coffee, tossing the red plastic stirrer aside. I deposited it in the trash and dabbed at the tiny mess he'd made.

"Quite a crowd," he said, taking a sip.

"It should be winding down soon." I thought of the pile of homework I'd be too exhausted to tackle by the time I was done cleaning up. "Calling hours end in twenty minutes. Good thing, too, since I don't think the Donohues can take much more."

"Or your boyfriend, either."

Boyfriend. Cute. I refused to give him the satisfaction of so much as a dirty look.

"It's getting to him." Henderson gestured with his coffee cup toward Matt. "You can tell."

Matt seemed fine to me. Noble, even. I was proud

of how he was lending an arm to Mrs. Donohue even though, in the end, Erin had treated him like dirt. It would have been easier for him to stay home, away from the stares and gossip. The boyfriend with the head injury.

"It'd be getting to me, too," I said, bending over to cinch up the trash, "if I was convinced everyone thought I was a murderer." I put aside the trash and shook out a new liner. "Like I told Detective Zabriskie earlier, the guy you should be investigating is Alex Bone. Or, as he was called in school, Stone Bone."

"How do you know we're not doing that already?"

"Because you're standing here talking to me and Zabriskie is flirting with my aunt."

I nodded to where the detective was in the corner having a heart-to-heart with Aunt Boo. He had one hand on the wall and was clearly laying on the charm.

Henderson was about to make a comment when he was suddenly blindsided by Sara's mother, Carol.

"Are you the off—" She blinked and gave it another go. "Are you the officer in charge of this investigation?"

The reek of alcohol rolling off Mrs. McMartin's tongue was so pungent, even Henderson had to take a few steps back. I couldn't believe it. The McMartins never drank anything stronger than root beer.

"And you are, ma'am?" Henderson asked.

"I am the daughter. I mean, I am the *mother* of a daughter, a girl, who lives in the very same neighborhood." Mrs. McMartin thrust out her arm, nearly smacking a mourner in the face. "The same neighborhood as Erin Donohue, and I want answers."

She swayed and was so loud, people were staring. Oh my God, I realized with mortification, Mrs. McMartin was *smashed*.

From across the room, Mom mouthed, "What's going on?"

I shrugged.

"This is supposed to be a safe community." Mrs. McMartin poked Henderson in the chest repeatedly. *Poke. Poke.* "You have the public trust, sir. The public trust!"

Sara appeared by the door, clutching her dwindling stack of memorial cards. Catching sight of her mother, she attempted to shoulder her way through the crowd.

"Coffee, Mrs. McMartin?" I offered, quickly pouring a cup.

"Yes," Henderson said between gritted teeth. "Ma'am, I do hope you have a designated driver this evening."

"Don't tell me what to designate," she said. "When the hell are you and your boys gonna put an end to this nightmare, detective? *When. The. Hell?*"

"Mom!" Sara arrived, almost breathless and nearly purple with humiliation. "Dad wants you. It's important."

With one last menacing glare, Mrs. McMartin toddled off under Sara's guidance. But soon there was another distraction. Kate Kline, who seconds before had been texting in line, was sobbing loudly over Erin's coffin.

"Man, does that break my heart," Zabriskie said, eating it up.

"Erin Donohue was her best friend," Henderson added. "Like a sister."

Matt and I made eye contact, and with a barely imperceptible twitching of his lips, he affirmed our mutual disgust for Kate, who capitalized on another's tragedy to make herself the center of attention.

Hooking the trash bag over one finger, I sidled out the door of Serenity, glad to escape the stifling room, the overpowering drama, and, worst of all, Kate Kline's sickening hypocrisy.

Unfortunately, stepping into the hall, I practically bumped into Sara and her mother.

"You're embarrassing me. Get a grip!" Sara hissed, as I attempted to inch past unnoticed.

I wanted to urge Sara not to be too hard on her

mother. Carol dipping into the cooking sherry was just another symptom of the disease that seemed to have infected Potsdam since Erin's death. Everyone was frantic for answers. It was a suicide. Then a murder. A random killer. Cops and metal detectors seemed to have established permanent residence at our school doors. ADT home security signs were popping up on lawns like mushrooms after a spring rain. And no one trusted anyone.

I never thought I'd say this, but I wished Potsdam was like it used to be: boring.

At the bottom of the service stairs, I opened a fire exit to the basement to dump the trash in the big bins and stopped short. A light was on in Boo's prep room.

Click!

Then it was off. A raven-haired girl backed out, closing the door softly behind her. Seeing me, she did a little skip.

"Oh!" Allie Woo exclaimed, clutching her rather large and beautiful pink Betsey Johnson bag.

"Were you looking for someone?" I asked.

"Not someone. Some *thing*. The bathroom. I was feeing sick again and couldn't wait. The lines for the ones upstairs are a mile long."

"Well, I hope you didn't barf in there," I said, dropping the trash. "Though, on second thought, I don't know why you couldn't. God knows there's been worse in that room."

Allie blanched, a reminder that not everyone was comfortable with funeral home shoptalk.

"There is another bathroom down here, but it's pretty utilitarian," I said, envisioning the dank space, with its hanging bulb, that only Manny used, and occasionally Boo. "Or you could come upstairs to our—"

"You mean that room I was in . . ." Allie thumbed over her shoulder. "That's where you . . ."

"Prep bodies, yes." I stated this with practiced dignity.

Even so, Allie went slightly green. "I've never been here before, so I didn't realize . . ."

"I know."

Like Erin, Cheyenne, and Kate, Allie was one of those girls whose mother politely called with some bogus excuse for missing my birthday parties—a soccer game, an incoming grandparent, possibly a cold.

"Wanna see where the magic happens?" I asked, daring her.

"Really?"

"Sure. Why not?" I opened Boo's door and flipped on the light to the spotless peach-and-white room. "Voila!"

Allie entered and shrank at the sight of the slightly

inclined stainless steel table at the center. "So that's for . . . ?"

"Prep. Usually what happens is Manny, our assistant, brings in the body and lays it on this table, which we keep very disinfected." I gave it a friendly pat. "We slip off the bag and then wash the body thoroughly. It's convenient because there's a drain right here, see?"

Allie peered at the drain. "That's where you substitute blood with . . ."

"Embalming fluid. We put it into this machine." I waved at the industrial-looking pump on the counter. "And then hook it up to an artery in the neck, if we're lucky. Sometimes, the body's not so intact and you've pretty much got to soak the remains in preservative." I waved to the cabinet of plastic Lithol bottles in a pink row.

"Normally, formaldehyde is colorless, a gas, actually. Formalin is the liquid mixture. Embalming fluid is a thicker version, and they add pink tint to improve the corpse's complexion." I read the bottle's description out loud. "'Ideal for the autopsied, electrified, frozen, or difficult to firm.'" It was what Boo used on Erin, but I kept that to myself.

"It's so weird that this is what your family does for a living and that you sleep right upstairs," Allie said, climbing onto the table.

It was the last thing I'd expected her to do. I mean, I would lie there all the time, especially in the summer when Boo cranked the air-conditioning in the prep room full blast. Then, the table was so nice and cold.

But Allie? No.

"I just wanted to know what it's like." She laid back and folded her hands in the traditional position, left over right. "We'll all end up here someday, right?"

"Possibly."

Allie closed her eyes and held her breath, a freaky imitation of a dead person. Except the dead aren't usually crying.

"Whoa!" I snatched a tissue and dabbed at the tears spilling from the corners of her eyes. "Are you all right?"

She shook her head. "No. Not at all. The sickness and sleeplessness haven't gotten any better." She brought her hand to her brow. "I'm not coping, Lily."

"Talk to me." This was my one window of opportunity and I had to make the most of it. "What happened at Erin's house Saturday night?"

Allie sighed feebly. "It was a big mistake that's going to haunt us for the rest of our lives."

She was driving me crazy. I needed facts, information, not weepy regrets—before someone found us in Boo's room. "Who was there?"

"The usual. Kate, Cheyenne, and me. And Erin, of course. We thought a party might lift her mood. She was a wreck because . . ." Allie hesitated.

"She was pregnant."

"No, she wasn't." Allie attempted a chuckle. "Where'd you hear that?"

"I read it on the death certificate—like you said, it was chock-full of mortician information—and Matt told me."

Allie sprang upright, her eyes wild. "He's not the father, just so you know. Erin and he never had . . ."

"Whatever. I'm not interested in Matt and Erin's sex life." Though I was, actually. "Go on. Why was she a wreck?"

"Aside from the obvious?" Allie went back to folding her arms. "Because instead of being sympathetic and loving, the guy who got her pregnant was pissed. He said he'd assumed she was on the pill and then he accused her of intentionally getting knocked up to get her hooks into him. He couldn't have been a bigger ass."

"Where did she meet this Prince Charming?"

Allie rolled to her side. "Maybe at the hospital where she interned last summer or the coffee shop where she used to get chai lattes. I'm not sure. Kate says he was way older and that's why she didn't go public, because if her parents found out she was dating someone out of high school they would have flipped."

They'd probably give anything for an older boyfriend to be the worst of their daughter's problems now, I thought.

"You told all this to the police, of course."

Allie bolted upright again. "No. And don't you, either. My God, Kate would kill me!"

"Who cares about Kate? Your friend was murdered."

"Except Kate says that if we come forward, the cops will interrogate us like they've been interrogating Matt, searching his lockers and house. And if they do that, then they might find out we were . . ." She balked.

"Drinking?"

"Well, that, but also . . ."

"Smoking . . . weed?"

"Um."

I wanted to slap her for being so coy. This was not a game. Lives were at stake. "Be specific."

"It was the kind of weed we did. We didn't know any better," she said sheepishly. "Erin was the only one of us who'd smoked before. And Kate, once, at her cousin's. Me? I never."

I was lost. "What was so special about this weed?"

"It was powerful, like it had been spiked. It wasn't

our fault. We thought it was Erin's, but she got it from Alex."

Alex Bone. I made a fist. I knew Stone Bone was somehow involved.

"As soon as we started smoking it, it was scary. It wasn't fun the way everyone said it would be. My skin started itching, like I couldn't stand being in it. I wanted to rip it off—it felt like bugs were underneath."

I shivered. What kind of pot would make you crawl out of your own skin? "Do you think it had PCP in it? Or, maybe, crack?"

"That's what Kate and I think," she said, nodding vehemently. "The thing is, we were so freaked, we left Erin alone, high on that stuff. And the next we heard, she was dead in her bathroom with slit wrists." Allie scrunched up her face into a wrinkled prune. "We killed her, Lily. I killed her."

I rewound those last two statements. "Did you just say you left her *alone*?"

"I know. We shouldn't have. You don't have to beat me up any more than I already am."

"No, what I mean is . . . Alex wasn't at the party?"

She wiped snot from under her nose. "Alex . . . Bone? Eww, no. We just smoked his weed. We didn't actually party with him."

I was so perplexed. Then who was the guy Erin had

been seen arguing with? Mrs. Krezky described someone like Matt. But he could have been the older guy
pretending to be younger by wearing a Panthers jacket.
A thought was making its way into my head no matter
how hard I tried to push it out.

There was a knock on the prep room door, followed
by Boo asking if I was in there.

"Just chatting," I said, shooing Allie off the table.
"Come on in."

Allie jumped to the floor and smoothed down her
dress. But not even our big, fake smiles could hide our
shock at the sight of Perfect Bob, flanked on either side
by uniformed and undercover officers wearing rubber
gloves and carrying plastic bags.

"They have a search warrant," Boo said quietly.
"There's nothing I can do to stop them."

Apparently, Bob had given Mom a heads-up about the
search as a courtesy, on the condition that she didn't
tell me and we didn't try to remove evidence. All Mom
had asked in return was for Bob and his force to hold
off until the wake was over, which they did—barely.

Allie went home along with the Donohues and
the other stragglers. Boo, Mom, Manny, Oma, and I
cleaned silently, sweeping up crumbs and doing dishes
while police officers trudged up and down the stairs. I

didn't stage a protest until one headed down the hall to my bedroom.

"What's he . . . ?" I said.

Mom put a finger to her lips. "He has a warrant. My hands are tied." She went down the hall to check anyway.

"Don't let them take my laptop," I called after her. "I still have a paper to write tonight."

"He's not going to take your laptop," Boo said, dumping a dustpan of dirt into the trash.

"How do you know?" I asked.

"Erwin told me."

Who was Erwin?

Oma shook suds off her hands. "Who's Erwin?"

"Detective Zabriskie." Boo acted as if this was no big deal. "Of the Pennsylvania State Police."

"My, my," Oma teased. "That's an even higher rank than Ruth's beau. She's slumming it with a rinky-dink police chief in comparison."

Manny laughed. "Undertakers and cops. Just figures. Stiffs like stiffs."

Boo flung a dishrag at his head, but he ducked, caught it, and tossed it back.

Mom returned to the kitchen and placed her hands on her hips. "I can hear you guys on the other side of the house. What's so funny?"

"Barbara has a boyfriend," Oma singsonged. "A statie, and you-oo don't."

"Zabriskie?" Mom said. "I saw you two talking. He's awfully short."

"Taller than you," said Boo.

Unfortunately, Bob stepped in just as Boo was accusing Mom of not liking any of the guys she dates. He cleared his throat. "We're done."

"What did you take?" Mom asked coldly.

"Not much. A couple of scalpels . . ."

"*My* scalpels?" Boo said, incensed. "What am I supposed to use?"

"I promise you'll get them back," Bob said. "We just need them for testing. And we wrote down the serial numbers of your embalming fluid."

"Why?" I asked.

"That's part of the investigation, Lily. I'm afraid I'm not at liberty to say."

I didn't understand why he needed the serial numbers of the embalming fluid until the following day.

But by then, regrettably, it was too late to help Allie Woo.

SIXTEEN

Can't pick u up 2 day.

Parents have gone mental

I stared at the message on my phone in bewilderment.
Sara had offered to drive me to school every day since the
day her license was six months old. This was so bizarre.

I texted back:

Are you skipping?

Sara wrote:

Today. And every day. Cant talk now. GTG

I got dressed in a daze, trying to remember the few instances when Sara and I hadn't been attached in school. On the rare occasions when she was sick, I barely knew how to function. Lunch was downright intolerable without her. That line about skipping school forever . . . She couldn't have been serious, right?

Then again, I'd called her the night before to tell her about the search and what Allie said and she didn't call back. Didn't text, either. So something definitely was up.

"What's wrong with you?" Mom asked when I dragged myself to the kitchen to pour a cup of coffee.

"Nothing." I listlessly added some cream.

"If this is nothing, I'd hate to see what something's like."

I put the cream back in the refrigerator and shut the door. "Sara just texted me that she can't pick me up this morning and oh, by the way, she's not going back to school. Ever."

Mom put her cup down so hard she spilled some over the edge. "You're kidding! What's that about?"

I popped an English muffin in the toaster. "Beats me."

"Do you think it has to do with the wake?"

"When Carol showed up drunk and started harassing Detective Henderson?"

"Is that what happened?" Mom shook her head.

"Ay yi yi. I thought the McMartins didn't drink alcohol."

"That's what I thought too."

My muffin popped up and I immediately slathered it with butter, despite my mother's insistence that her vegan spread was a healthier choice. If there was such a thing as vegan kale-almond butter, Mom and Perfect Bob would buy it by the case.

Mom didn't give my English muffin a second glance, though. She was staring at her manicured pink nails, thinking.

"Might be better if you give Sara some space," she said quietly. "The family might be having issues."

"What kind of issues?" I said, biting into the buttery bready goodness.

Mom leaned over and pinched my lips closed. "Grown-up issues. And please, try to remember not to talk with your mouth full."

With Erin's funeral scheduled for 11:00 a.m. the next day, Mom couldn't spare thirty minutes in her busy schedule to drive me to school, though personally I think she derived secret pleasure in making me walk two miles to the city bus.

I didn't actually mind the walk and, begrudgingly, I admitted that my mother's fanaticism for fresh air and exercise had its benefits. The air was crisp from last night's snow, and where shadows darkened the sidewalks there were slippery patches. But it was decidedly sunnier, which helped lift my mood as well as improve my ability to notice the silver sedan parked at the bottom of the hill.

It could have been the paranoia that seemed to have seeped into all our pores since Erin's murder. Sure. It also could have been the same car that had been following Sara and me earlier in the week.

At Elm, I took a chance and crossed at the red, not daring to look back as I heard the crunch of gravel and the distinct squeal of wheels turning in a U-ey. A horn beeped. Twice. I ignored it and cut through the backyard of an old red Victorian house and then down a driveway until I ended up on Laurel.

Safe at last, I tugged my backpack over my shoulder and was about to step off the curb when a blue pickup came careening over the hill and braked to a stop.

Matt leaned across the seat. "What's wrong with you?"

"What's wrong with *you*?" I said, gasping. "That was almost a hit-and-run."

"Don't be dramatic. Get in," he said, opening the door. "What were you doing running like a scared chicken?"

I clicked my seat belt. "I was not a scared chicken. Someone was following me."

"Yeah, me." He shifted into first, checked his mirror, and shook his head. "It's never a dull moment with you, Lily."

"Why were you looking for me, anyway?" I asked as we bumped and bounced down Laurel, a road not famous for its smooth surface.

"Sara called and said I had to pick you up."

That was a shocker. I didn't even know she had his number. "Since when did you two become buddies?"

"Since she told me at the wake last night that you met up with Alex Bone." He wagged a finger. "That dude is bad news. I've been doing some checking, Lil. Did you know he served time?"

"He let that drop in the conversation, yes."

"For assault. He's violent."

I stared out the window, debating whether to relay what Allie said about Erin hooking up with an older guy.

"Also, he deals," Matt said. "Nasty stuff that can mess you up permanently."

I spun around. "What do you mean?"

"It's not even weed, what he sells. They're just regular cigarettes laced with something. Jacks tried one at a party and said he spent the rest of the night on the couch having a conversation—with himself."

One Jacks was bad enough. "And he got it from Alex?"

"Bought it at the coffee shop. Jacks told me he literally stepped outside of his body and he was like two people. Never wanted to do that again."

Exactly what Allie had said. We turned the corner to the school and saw the blue flashing light of the cop car in the distance. "Was it PCP?"

"Have no idea. Whatever it is, it's called wet."

At that moment, I had an out-of-body experience of my own. "Stop! Now!"

Matt yanked the wheel to the right and drove off the road. "You okay?"

"No. No, I am absolutely not okay," I said, gripping my stomach. Oh, this was bad. Really, really bad. "Okay, so, our insurance company has been after us to install a security camera in the prep room."

"You made me stop to talk insurance?"

"Listen. All the funeral homes are doing it now. You know why? Because there've been so many break-ins by kids stealing embalming fluid. And do you know why they're stealing embalming fluid?" I didn't wait for his response. "Because it is mostly formalin and formalin is what you need to make wet weed. They soak weed in the stuff, then dry and sell it for huge profits."

Matt nodded. "And this, I'm guessing, is why they call it wet."

"I think that's what Allie, Kate, and Cheyenne were smoking with Erin the night she was murdered."

He went white. "You're telling me that Erin, who could barely handle a sip of communion wine, was smoking *wet*?" He frowned. "Bull."

"That's what Allie said. Also, the cops searched our house last night and took down the serial numbers of the embalming fluid." I realized then that this meant the cops thought I was the supplier. "Like I was in on it."

"You'll be okay," Matt said calmly, stroking my arm. "We're getting closer to finding out who did this and you know the cops are, too."

I said, "Yeah. You're right."

We were both becoming expert liars.

Matt dropped me off at the bus stop so the cops wouldn't see us arriving in the same vehicle. It was totally inane, this business of going through the metal detector and being searched, and it didn't solve anything. The murderer wasn't going to show up at school with a kit of knives and drugs.

If the murderer had been lost in a formalin-induced psychosis, he might not even have remembered what he did.

This was a perfect example of why I could not exist without Sara. No doubt somewhere in the recesses of her vast knowledge of cheesy true crimes, there was a case she'd watched about some fool out of his brain on wet, slicing and dicing a person to pieces.

I tried her cell and got no answer. Then I made the mistake of sending her the following text:

Have lead on E's murder. When can we talk?

Two minutes later, I got this strangely formal response:

Hello, Lily. Dr. Ken and I have decided to suspend Sara's account. She won't need it for a while. I'm sure you'll receive a good old-fashioned letter in the mail explaining all. God bless. Mrs. M.

First off, who texted like that, in complete sentences with punctuation and everything? Second off, Sara wouldn't need a phone for a while? What did that mean? And what was her mother doing reading and replying to her texts?

Homeschooling. Ugh. I bet that's what the McMartins were planning. Poor Sara, stuck at the kitchen table memorizing psalms or whatever.

After sitting through a particularly grueling calculus class, I made the executive decision to blow off the rest of the day and devote my energy to getting to the bottom of this wet weed business. The cops were obviously barking up the wrong tree if they were raiding Boo's supplies in an effort to implicate me. And I certainly wasn't about to let them steamroll Matt and me into some Bonnie-and-Clyde murder rap.

The key, I concluded, was cajoling Kate and her groupies into fessing up to the police, though this was against their selfish interests. College season was upon us, and "I got stoned on wet with my best friend the night she was murdered" was not exactly the dream beginning to an admissions essay.

But I would make them see otherwise. The trick would be to approach them individually, when they would be more vulnerable to suggestion.

As luck would have it, opportunity knocked during second period when I came down the stairs of the atrium to find Kate Kline with her surgically improved nose in a World Cultures textbook, alone and out of sight, on a couch reserved for seniors.

"Hello," I said, flopping down next to her. "Long time, no see."

She was not nearly as delightful as she'd been at the

wake. "Buzz off, freak. I have a quiz next period."

"My, that's not very friendly." I peeked over her shoulder. She was reading a passage about Chinese family life. "The Chinese have totally messed-up death rituals," I said. "Did you know if you die single, your family just leaves you at the funeral home because you're considered worthless? Also, if anything in the color red comes in contact with the body before it's buried, that person becomes a ghost. They believe ghosts are everywhere."

Kate lowered her book. "And you wonder why you don't have more friends."

"Oh, not that much." I did a quick scan for her henchwomen. "Where's your entourage?"

"Skipping school. Where's your deformed twin?"

I clucked my tongue. "You know, you won't be able to keep up this politically incorrect dialogue once you're out of Potsdam."

She went back to reading. "Bye-bye."

"Though I suppose leaving Potsdam isn't really happening for you, is it? Considering."

Kate sighed and said, "All right. I'll bite. What's up?"

"I need you to go to the cops," I said. "And tell them what happened Saturday night."

"Not that it's any of your business, but I've already

been interviewed by the police."

"Sure. But I don't think you told them everything."

Kate closed her book. "Like what?"

"Like the fact that you, Cheyenne, and Allie were smoking . . ."

"We smoked weed once," she cut in, checking over her shoulder. "It was just a coincidence that Erin got . . . you know. And what do you care?"

"I care because you weren't smoking weed. What you were smoking was Alex Bone's concoction of cigarettes and embalming fluid, which produces a cheap, brain-bending, psychotic high with huge profit margins for Stone Bone Enterprises."

Kate swallowed. I'd really caught her by surprise with that one. Or so I thought, until she said, "Embalming fluid? That is so gross."

I shrugged. "Depends what you're using it for."

"It wasn't embalming fluid," she said with disgust. "The weed was soaked in *formaldehyde*. Erin brought home a bottle from the hospital. It's not illegal or anything. You can buy it off the internet."

"You mean *Erin* made the wet?"

Kate curled the corner of her lip. "I love how you keep saying 'wet,' like this is *Breaking Bad*. You're such a nerd, Lily."

Yes, I thought, but at least I didn't go around

inhaling formaldehyde, a known carcinogen linked to fifteen different types of cancers. Not that I was about to point this out to Kate, since that would have only been more nerdlike.

"Okay," I said. "So if it wasn't illegal, and Erin got it from her summer internship at the hospital and borrowed a bottle of formalin like you borrow paper clips and rubber bands from the office, then you won't have any problem telling that to the police."

Kate went back to her book. "See ya!"

"You need to come forward about this and what you know about Erin's baby daddy."

She kept on reading.

"Because you don't want that guilt for the rest of your life. Erin was your best friend, and if I know anything about the dead, it's that they demand justice. She's watching you, Kate, and waiting for you to do right by her. Or else."

I left Miss Kline to stew about that for a while. My words might have gone in one ear and out the other, but I had reason to hope. As I walked up the stairs, I peered over the banister and saw she was still staring at that passage about Chinese family culture.

Ghosts. The Chinese weren't so far off about them being everywhere.

* * *

The Sara thing was really getting to me. All morning, I'd had the feeling that I was forgetting something, and then I'd remember . . . it was my best friend. There was no one to relate, detail by detail, the deliciousness of my juicy encounter with Kate Kline, no one to analyze the wet weed twist with or trade notes with in physics. I even missed her occasionally tedious rundowns of criminal cases gone wrong.

Finally, at lunch, I couldn't take it anymore. I found Matt and asked him to give me a lift downtown to Boo's salon so I could borrow her car and go to Sara's. The only problem there was because I was still seventeen, I had to hide in the back until Matt showed his ID, proving he was eighteen and therefore a legal adult who was free to leave school property without parental approval.

"This is getting old, very fast," I said, crawling out of the back to the shotgun seat.

Matt gripped the wheel. He looked troubled.

I said, "What's happened now?"

"It's probably nothing, but I got a text from Allie when I was walking out to the parking lot. All it said was, 'I'm sorry.'"

"Good. She should be sorry. Kate's convinced her that if they go to the cops and tell them what happened Saturday night their lives will be ruined." I threw up my hands in helplessness. "Doesn't matter that your life will be ruined and possibly mine . . ."

He ran a hand through his hair, standing it on end. Football season was almost through, and I was dying for it to be long again. Not a fan of the military look.

"I'm still going to check on her after practice. She wasn't in school today and she hasn't been herself lately."

That was nice of him. Maybe too nice. "Um, is there a thing going on between you and . . ."

He turned to me, exasperated. "Geesh, Graves. You have a habit of underestimating yourself, don't you?"

"No." To be quite honest, I'd often worried that I had too much self-esteem, if that was even possible.

"Then, what is it?" he asked. "Don't you like me?"

Now, I was completely confused. "I think we're having two different conversations simultaneously."

We got to the corner of Main and Pine and I said he could let me off there. As I hopped out of the truck and thanked him for the lift, Matt leaned over and said, "Someday this whole nightmare's going to be over and then . . ."

"Yeah?"

He shook his head. "Forget it. Talk to you later." He pulled into the Dunkin' Donuts so he could head back to school. I watched him go and smiled all the way to Boo's.

* * *

Boo's salon was one of three in downtown Potsdam, distinguished only by the fact that its awning was green while the other two were white. Its plate-glass storefront featured bottles of sun-faded hair products and pictures of women glancing down and to the side modestly so you'd focus on their unmanageably nineties styles.

A bell tinkled when I opened the door to a haze of hair spray and chatter. Boo was one of the more colorful stylists, seeing as how she was covered head to toe in tats, and one of the more popular, too. Friday was her busiest day, but that didn't stop her from giving me a big hug and telling me to take a seat in the free chair next to her station.

She was finishing up a perm on ninety-year-old Mrs. D'Angelo, who would likely end up on Boo's *other* workstation in the not too distant future. This was a more common pattern than people knew in Potsdam, especially among Boo's regulars. They'd trusted her to make them look their best when they were alive, why should it be any different when they died?

"School out already?" Boo asked. Then, checking the clock on the wall and seeing it was only twelve thirty, she said, "Lily. We've been over this. You promised to stop cutting."

I twirled in the chair. "I have a crisis, and I can't concentrate."

She sighed. "Okay, let's situate Mrs. D'Angelo under the dryer and we'll get a cup of coffee."

Mrs. D'Angelo picked up right where their conversation had ended when I'd apparently interrupted, therefore I was treated to a recitation of complaints—why jars were *so* hard to open these days, how kids were *so* obsessed with electronics they couldn't communicate with fellow humans, and what a shame it was that the one good teenage girl in town had to meet such a brutal end.

"She went to my church and she was an angel," Mrs. D'Angelo gushed. "I didn't think they made them like that these days."

I fingered the pentagram at my neck. Boo gave me a wink.

Once Mrs. D'Angelo was set up with her *Us* and *Family Circle* magazines, along with a cup of weak tea, Boo wiggled her finger for me to join her in the back. There were a couple of stools there and a washer/dryer that was forever spinning towels. Boo dropped a tiny plastic coffee cartridge into the Keurig and said, "Hazelnut?"

"Sure." I took one of the stools as Boo popped open

a box of chamomile tea for herself and plugged in the electric kettle. Girl was old school.

"Spill," she said, handing me a paper cup of coffee. "What's so distracting that you have to leave school?"

"Nothing much. Just a girl getting murdered."

She gave me a look. "Fortunately for you, my twelve thirty's late, so cut to the chase."

I told her about Sara and what Mom had said about giving her space. "Does your mom know about the text Carol sent?"

"No." I watched while Boo fixed herself a cup of chamomile. "Should that matter?"

Boo poured hot water over her teabag. "Look. You know your mother and I have different philosophies about what you need." She unplugged the kettle and turned to me. "At the end of the day, she is your mother and her word goes."

"I sense a *but* here somewhere."

"*Buuuut*, if it were me and my lifelong friend suddenly cut off contact, I think I'd go over to her house and see what's up."

This was such a relief. "I was thinking the same thing. I mean, I can understand why her parents want to keep her out of school. It's crazy there with the cops and metal detectors. But there's no reason we can't see each other, right?"

"Right." Boo dumped her teabag in the trash.

"And I really do need to talk to her about why Perfect Bob took down the serial numbers on the embalming fluid bottles."

Boo's pierced eyebrow arched over the rim of her teacup as she took a sip. "You have a theory about that, huh?"

I told her what Allie said about the bad high and the wet weed and how Kate had confirmed Erin had stolen formalin from the hospital.

The teacup nearly fell from Boo's hand. I caught it as it slipped out of her grasp, tea all over her apron.

"Oh," she whispered, bringing her delicate fingers to her lips. "Oh, no."

I'd never seen my aunt so flustered. Usually she was cool as a cucumber. I grabbed a wad of paper towels and dabbed the tea off her front. The bell tinkled and in stepped a young woman in skirt and heels, obviously on her lunch hour. Boo's twelve thirty.

"I've got to go," Boo said, brushing back her hair and checking her reflection in the mirror.

"Wait!" I caught hold of her elbow before she could escape. "Tell me."

"I can't, Lily. I'm sorry. Your mother . . ." Boo's lovely blue eyes watered. Clearly this was killing her.

Gripping her by the shoulders, I said, "Matt's

future is at stake. Mine, too. Erin's dead. This is not the moment to be keeping secrets."

Boo held up a finger to show her twelve thirty she'd be right there. "Okay. I'll tell you. But I need you to swear you won't breathe a word to anyone else."

I crossed my heart.

"This is going to be upsetting for you, but when Erin arrived for prepping, there were several anomalies I had to fix."

"Okay." So far, so good. Pretty routine.

"For example, her nostrils were filled with blood. I had to clean those out and plug them, and it wasn't easy. But the worst was the interior of her mouth. I had a dickens of a time weaving the wires through her gums because they had simply rotted away."

I wasn't following. "Why would her gums have been rotted?"

"For the same reason that her tongue was black and the inside of her mouth was gray and why, when I zipped open the body bag, I had to grab a mask and cover my mouth and nose because she so reeked of formaldehyde."

"Formaldehyde?" I said, puzzled. "*Before* you embalmed her?"

Boo nodded. "That's how she died. Not from blood loss. Not from overdosing on wet whatever, but from someone pouring embalming fluid down her throat."

I gasped, unable to imagine a more awful death. "And that's why the cops searched our stuff."

"And why Bob wants to name you as a suspect. Guess he's not so perfect after all, huh?"

SEVENTEEN

That explained why Mom had been so cold to Bob after the search, because according to Boo they were "on hiatus" until this case was over. Part of me felt crummy for ruining Mom's love life. Despite all the teasing I gave them for running together and being kale-munching, yoga-practicing health nuts, they made a cute couple.

The other part of me thought Bob was a jerk for even considering that I was capable of murder. And not just any murder, either. Death by formaldehyde. Seriously, I would never forgive him.

Boo loaned me her car so I could go to Sara's. First, however, I walked down to my old haunt, the Potsdam

Public Library—a place I would always associate with falling in love.

In my fear of leaving a digital trail, I was pretty skittish about checking out medical journals on formaldehyde or Googling the term on my iPhone, so I logged on anonymously to one of the public computers instead. What I discovered was so horrifying that a librarian shushed me when I involuntarily let out a cry of horror.

Apparently, formalin was only 4 percent formaldehyde, a naturally occurring gas that's soluble in water. The rest of the solution is methanol and other compounds to keep it stable. It is used mostly in laboratories and hospitals to "fix"—or pickle—nonliving organisms, and in morticians' prep rooms for the same reason. It also kills bacteria and was once widely used as a disinfectant until people caught on that they were wiping poison all over the place.

If ingested in large amounts, it could lead to intense pain, violent convulsions, coma, and eventually death. Even worse, formalin corroded the mouth on contact, instantly killing all taste buds, before it went on to shred the esophagus and pulverize the stomach and intestines. For that reason, it was rarely used in suicides because death by formalin was such a painful process. The overpowering noxious odor alone was enough to deter most people from getting their noses near it.

I covered my face with my hands, willing the world to stop spinning. Obviously, Erin hadn't consumed the formalin willingly or even accidentally. The killer had poured it down her throat, as Boo said. Had he held a gun to her head? Or did he employ another threat?

Enough. I logged off and went to find Sara.

My goal was to catch her at home alone before Carol returned from getting Brandon at the elementary school. However, the house was closed up when I pulled into the driveway. The garage door was down and the blinds were drawn on the first-floor windows. Weird.

I rang the doorbell anyway, twice. It was a big house and Sara could have been in the TV den at the far back, or taking a shower. On the third *ding-dong*, I was rewarded with the sound of heavy footsteps crossing the foyer.

The door swung open and there stood Dr. Ken on the other side of the glass storm door, in his white lab coat, merrily colored bow tie knotted under his black beard.

"Hi!" I said, waving. "Is Sara in?"

He made no move to open the door. "I'm sorry, but Sara's not here. She's at the doctor."

It hadn't occurred to me until then that Sara might have been sick, that she was suffering from some dreadful illness she'd bravely been keeping to herself. I recalled Mom's warning that I should give the McMartins space because they were dealing with issues, and instantly regretted barging over here to share a piece of gossip.

"Oh, wow. I had no idea. Is she going to be okay?" I asked.

I must have looked pitiful on the doorstep, near tears at the imminent death of my best and—let's face it—only true friend, because Dr. Ken finally opened the door and said, "Come on in, Lily. And I'll explain."

We walked through the huge foyer to the kitchen, with its familiar black granite counters and sparkling white cabinets. Dr. Ken went to the sink and poured a glass of water. "You might need this," he said, leading me to the great room.

I sat on the edge of their pristine white couch and clutched my glass. Whatever Sara was facing, I would be with her every step of the way. I sucked my lower lip and tried to channel strength. God, this had been an awful week.

Dr. Ken smiled. "It's okay, Lily. Sara's fine."

"You mean she doesn't have cancer or something?"

He seemed amused. "Heavens no. Sara's incredibly healthy."

I pondered the water. "Then what do I need this for?"

"Because you're in for a bit of a surprise." He leaned forward, hands clasped between his knees. "The reason Sara's at the doctor's is so she can get her vaccinations." He smiled broadly. "We're going on a mission to India! Isn't it wonderful?"

"What?" Sara never mentioned going to India. Then I realized he meant the rest of the family, because she needed to stay here in Potsdam and finish senior year.

"When did you decide this?" I asked, taking a sip.

"Last spring. That's why Sara applied early decision to Yale, so she could get that admissions gobbledygook out of the way and be free to leave during Christmas vacation."

"Oh, I get it," I said, much more relieved. "You guys are going to India for a mission and Sara's visiting you over Christmas vacation. Cool."

He shook his head. "No. We are a family and families stick together, Lily. We had planned on leaving at the end of the year, but after this outburst of violence in the community, Carol and I thought maybe we should expedite the trip. We've been urging Sara to break the news to you so it wouldn't be such a shock, but . . ."

I put the glass on a coaster, my hand shaking. "Wait. Are you telling me you're taking Sara three thousand miles away from here?"

"Four thousand. But we'll be back next summer."

My head started to pound. I wanted this to be a Dr. Ken wacky practical joke, for him to jump up and say, "April Fools!" even though it was November.

"Gee whiz, Lily," he said. "It's not the end of the world. You can stay in touch, maybe not digitally, but last I checked the old mail system still worked."

I breathed in and out. He was serious. I couldn't believe it. "How soon are you going?"

"Well, our church is throwing us a farewell potluck brunch on Sunday and from there we'll drive to JFK and take a six-thirty flight to Delhi."

This wasn't happening. They couldn't take Sara away from me. I got up and for some reason went to the kitchen. Then returned to the great room. It was like my legs wouldn't let me stay still.

"Dr. Ken. You don't understand. I need Sara."

"I understand," he said, closing his eyes. "And Sara needs you. But it's not forever. Like I said, she'll be back by the fall."

That was no good. "By next fall, she'll be in college and I'll be . . . here!"

"Lily, please sit."

I couldn't. I folded my arms and positioned myself in front of the fireplace while Dr. Ken looked up at me pleadingly. "It's only for ten months."

"I just don't see why you have to go now."

"You're not a parent, so you don't know what Carol and I have been going through. Erin interned in my office for six weeks and we really got to know her as a fine, moral girl. For Carol and me, the similarities between her and Sara are too close for comfort."

I couldn't think of two more opposite people. Did Dr. Ken even know his daughter or how she'd been mercilessly taunted by "fine, moral" Erin all through grade school?

"Both Erin and Sara are sweet girls who love God," he continued. "They are innocents."

Granted, Potsdam High might have been right up there with Sodom and Gomorrah, but he definitely didn't know his daughter if he thought Sara was an innocent.

"When Erin was found dead—*murdered*—a mere hop and a skip from our house, it shattered our perception that this neighborhood was a sanctuary." Dr. Ken stroked his beard. "I'm sorry, Lily, but I would rather subject my children to the known challenges of poverty and disease while serving the Lord, than let them succumb to the unknown temptations of a secular society."

He sighed. "And those true-crime shows I know

Sara's watching on her computer late at night while we're in bed . . . they are so unhealthy."

Perhaps if I could reason with him . . . , I thought. "You're wrong about Erin being like Sara, Dr. Ken. Erin was into way more stuff than anyone suspected. She was hanging out with a dealer named Stone Bone, who was a bad influence. I don't want to blame the victim, but Sara is not Erin. She's got a good head on her shoulders."

Dr. Ken tented his hands as if in prayer. "Erin made all the right choices."

"She didn't." I resented being put in a position where I was making it seem like Erin had gotten herself murdered. "But it doesn't matter what choices she made."

He dropped his hands, surprised. "Lily, God gave Man free will as a test. Making the right choices is what keeps us out of temptation."

"Then God's an idiot," I spat, "if He let Erin be murdered as a so-called test."

The cheeks above Dr. Ken's beard inflamed with anger. "I like you, Lily, but you need to respect my beliefs. What you just said is sacrilege."

I closed my eyes, trying to stay focused. "My point is, you can't protect your daughter by sending her to India. Only Sara can protect herself."

"That's not true." He stood, clearly fed up with our conversation. "I can protect Sara. And I will. I am, after all, her father." He walked to the door and opened it. "If you don't mind, there is a lot of packing I need to finish, as well as praying to do for your soul."

I got up and went to the door. Only then did I notice the suitcases and boxes lined up on one side of the foyer. This was really happening. They were taking Sara away from me.

Forever.

That evening, I drove through the gloaming like I'd just lost my best friend. Which I had. It was the unfairness of the situation that riled me the most. Sara was almost eighteen, an adult. Who were the McMartins to make an arbitrary ruling that she had to follow them halfway around the world?

I was so upset by this that I forgot Boo was at work and drove straight home, parking her car at its usual spot in front of the carriage house before traipsing through the garden to the back door. Oma was at the stove, standing on a stool and stirring a pot.

"You're home early," she said, laying down the spoon as I slumped into a kitchen chair. "How did the physics quiz go?"

I shook my head. "Blew it off."

"Oh, dear, Lily. You have to stop doing that." Oma found a tin of cookies and offered me a chewy molasses one, her specialty and usually my favorite. But I had no appetite.

Mom came bustling in holding the guest book from last night. "I thought I heard you in those awful boots. Do you have any idea what this means?" She pointed to an entry beside Alex Bone's name, written in dramatic cursive. It said:

You took something of mine. Give it back.

An hour before, that would have given me the chills. But now, after learning about what they were doing to Sara, nothing mattered. Not even Stone Bone. "He's a twit, Mom. Ignore it."

"That's odd," Oma said, reading over my shoulder. "Usually people write 'So sorry for your loss' or 'Our prayers and thoughts are with you.'"

"What does it mean?" Mom asked again.

"It means that Alex Bone is a loser drug addict who only thinks about himself." I closed the book and put my head on the table.

They wouldn't even let me talk to Sara. They probably wouldn't even let me say good-bye. Probably they thought I was the one leading her into temptation.

I felt a slight hand on my shoulder and smelled the distinctive scent of rose perfume. "Can you give us a minute, Oma?" Mom said.

After Oma left, Mom pulled out a chair and sat next to me, fingering the hair on my forehead, straightening it like she used to do when I was a little girl. "You went to the McMartins', didn't you?"

I nodded and braced for the inevitable I-told-you-so.

"Sara should have said something sooner. Ken told me last night that he and Carol had planned this last spring. They would have left during the summer if Sara hadn't needed to do college interviews."

I had to admit that it felt nice to have Mom's sympathy. "It sucks."

"I know and, personally, I think it's a mistake. Second semester senior year is the fun semester. Sara's going to be missing out on so much." Mom handed me a tissue. This was one of her magic skills, pulling Kleenex out of nowhere.

"What am I going to do?" I said, blowing my nose. "It just won't be the same without her."

"You'll do what you've always done, Lily. You'll be yourself and let others come to you. That's what you did with Sara and . . ."

I said, "Matt."

Mom sighed. "You two have been seeing each other behind my back, haven't you?"

"You wouldn't let me see him in front of your back, so . . ." I smiled. "Anyway, he really is a good guy. He's not who you think, and trust me, he had nothing to do with Erin's death."

"Maybe you're right," she said slowly. "However, this town wants an arrest and I'm afraid if they don't get one soon, there's going to be a riot."

The office phone rang. Oma picked it up.

"Whoever did it was older and got Erin pregnant," I said. "And he probably forced her to drink . . ." I caught myself in the nick of time. ". . . *poison* that caused her to die fairly quickly. Then the murderer staged it so it looked like a suicide."

"Alex Bone?" Mom said.

"You've been talking to Bob."

"No," she said. "I've been listening to you."

Oma entered clutching the phone to her chest, her eyes gleaming. "It's for you, Lily. It's a boy!"

I took the phone. My grandmother was so silly when it came to the opposite sex.

"Hey," Matt said, sounding urgent. "Where are you? I didn't want to call your cell phone."

"I'm at home."

"Okay, I'm right around the corner." Then he hung

up without so much as a good-bye.

I stared at the receiver. "It was Matt. Sounded important."

"Hot date?" asked Oma.

"I don't think so," I said, as his blue truck careened into the driveway. We watched through the kitchen window as Matt leaped out and rushed to the door, banging three times.

Mom opened it and regarded him levelly. "You must be the infamous Matt Houser."

He extended his hand. "Hello, Mrs. Graves. Nice to meet you. I like your daughter. She has my utmost respect. I have never, nor would I ever, harm anyone. On that you have my word. I did not murder Erin, nor do I know who did. But right now, if you don't mind, I need Lily. It's an emergency."

Matt reached around Mom and extended his hand. I took it.

EIGHTEEN

"It's Allie," he said, taking shortcuts to the west side of town. "I called her when I got out of practice. She sounded loaded."

I gripped the side of the car as we pushed fifty in a thirty-five-mile-an-hour zone. "Every ten miles of speeding only buys you one minute," I said.

"And in this case, every minute counts."

"Where are the other Tragically Normals?"

"Who?"

"Kate and Cheyenne."

He shrugged. "Let's hope they're at Allie's house, because from the way she was sounding, she should not be alone."

Darkness came early these days, and when we arrived at Allie's house, the sun was over the horizon and the streetlights were on. Matt took my hand and together we rushed up Allie's brick-and-white colonial home. There were no cars in the driveway, no sign of parents.

"You sure she's here?" I asked, following him around to the back after the doorbell got us nowhere.

"She said she was home." Cupping his hands on a downstairs window, he peered in and said, "The TV's on."

I tried opening the sliding door, but it was locked. Every door was locked.

"I wish you'd heard her, Graves. It was like she was possessed. Kept talking about people watching her and there being no safe place for any of us and how all the walls were crumbling down." He backed up to examine the upper windows. "She sounded so much like Erin. Paranoid."

I had a flash memory of Allie turning off the light and quietly exiting Boo's prep room. That big Betsey bag. Ugh. Why didn't I think to check it? "Matt, we have to get in there. Or call 911. She might have taken something bad."

"Like what?"

"Just . . . call her. I'll tell you later."

Matt tried calling her on his phone. No answer. Then, placing two fingers in his mouth, he produced a whistle of such high-pitched frequency that he could have set off alarms.

"Allie? You in? It's me, Matt."

A light flicked on and the curtains at an upstairs window parted slightly. A silhouette of a girl with long, dark hair appeared. Talk about ghostly.

Matt cupped his hands to his mouth. "Open up, Allie."

She shook her head slowly and let the curtains fall.

In frustration, Matt tried the sliding door again, while I headed around the house to the garage, finding one of the two doors unlocked. Lifting it open, I fumbled for a light and yelled for Matt.

"Awesome," he said. "I've been in this house before. That door in the corner leads to the kitchen."

I went over to the door and turned the handle, and much to my relief, it opened. We ran in, shouting Allie's name.

He dashed up the stairs while I turned on lights. Everything appeared to be in order. I wondered when her parents would be home and what could be the reason for Allie's odd behavior.

Matt reached the landing and froze. Allie was singing. Or crying. It was hard to tell. "Oh my God. Lily," he said. "Come here quick!"

I found him standing in the doorway of Allie's bedroom, and there on the floor, next to a pile of clothes, was Allie Woo, pale, bloodied, and meticulously braiding her hair.

She lifted her gaze to me with dull, faraway eyes. "Oh, good, you came, Lily. I was so hoping you'd join us."

My hand reached for Matt, who gave me a be-strong squeeze before letting go and squatting next to Allie. "What's up?"

She giggled.

The room was a disaster, as if Allie had emptied every drawer and her entire closet of their contents. Dresses lay ripped to shreds. Heels were broken off their shoes. A pair of pink underwear dangled from a ceiling fan.

Allie curled into a fetal position and began rocking.

"We need to call an ambulance," I whispered. "She's cut herself." I pointed to the floor where a large maroon stain was spreading over the cream-colored carpet.

"Jesus," Matt said, looking rather sick himself. "Allie. Why'd you do this?"

"You can't call the police," Allie said. "They'll just arrest you."

There was some truth to that, I thought, taking out my phone and dialing 911 anyway. And that probably explained why Kate and Cheyenne were staying away.

Some friends.

The dispatcher got on and I gave her Allie's name and approximate address. Then I gave ours: Lily Graves and Matt Houser.

"There's a suicide attempt," I said. "Come quick."

I described the scene as best as I could—possible drugs or intoxication, a seventeen-year-old girl, approximately one hundred and fifteen pounds and kind of out of it.

Matt held up her wrists to display superficial horizontal cuts. Enough to cause a lot of capillary bleeding and tons of pain, but not life-threatening.

I covered the receiver and said, "Tourniquet."

He ripped a strip of white cotton from an already destroyed T-shirt and tied it at her right elbow, pulling it tightly. Then he did the same to her left. Allie, meanwhile, had gone limp, her arms flopping to the side.

"Do you think she's going to make it?" he asked, cradling her.

I put my nose to her mouth.

"What are you doing?" Matt asked.

"Sniffing for formaldehyde." I exhaled in relief. "Vodka. And plenty of it."

"Allie. Why?" He brushed back her hair, much like my mother had done for me only minutes before. "You're better than this."

But Allie was out cold. I put two fingers to her neck and felt for a pulse that was stronger than I'd expected.

"She feels guilty. She blames herself for something that's not her fault." I lifted my fingers from her neck and touched his cheek. "You know what that's like, right?"

Matt nodded and stroked Allie's shoulder. "It's not your fault. You did nothing wrong. You have to let it go and go on the best you can."

He could have been advising himself.

Red and white lights flashed in the hallway. I ran downstairs and unlocked the front door for a crew of emergency technicians who arrived with radios crackling.

"She's upstairs," I said.

A woman in a white EMT uniform took me aside. "Wait here. We'll need to ask a few questions."

After several minutes, Matt came down and folded his arms. They were splotched with blood. "They're taking care of her. I think she'll be okay."

"Absolutely," I said, rubbing his back. "It was great the way you were talking to her. I'm sure she heard you."

"I hope so. I'm sick of all this death and cutting." Impulsively, he wrapped me in a hug and said, "Don't you start freaking out too, okay?"

"Come on." I tried to make light of it, but the truth was that I had fallen for Matt Houser. Hard. I liked that he'd been a good enough friend of Allie's to check on her after practice, that he didn't flinch at blood or hesitate when it came to doing what he could to stem the bleeding. But mostly I liked that he was holding me tight and, every once in a while, brushing his lips against my hair.

"Hey," he murmured, "you're shaking."

Was I? I didn't like to consider myself the quivering female. Then again, there was something about being with Matt that allowed me to unravel. He was strong and he understood what I was going through. I wanted to lean against him and bury my face in his neck, to forget the blood and violence of the past few days. And I might have done just that if Detective Zabriskie hadn't chosen that moment to walk through the front door.

He took one glance at us in a clutch and said, "Why am I not surprised?"

Matt said, "Take it easy, dude. This time we're the good guys."

* * *

Allie was transported to Potsdam Regional Medical Center. I overheard the EMT tell Zabriskie that she appeared to be suffering from acute alcohol intoxication and would be fine after she had her stomach pumped, though she might be admitted to the psych ward overnight for observation. Her parents, at a fundraiser one town over, had been notified and were on their way.

After Matt and I gave our written statements and we were driving back to my house, I had a thought.

"Do you have Kate Kline's number?"

Matt reached in his pocket and handed his phone to me. "Here. Why?"

"She won't listen to me, but she'll listen to you." I looked up her number. "When she gets on, tell her that Allie tried to kill herself tonight and that the cops are at the hospital where Erin wants her and Cheyenne to go and do the right thing."

"Erin?" Matt grimaced. "She's dead."

"In body only. In Kate's imagination, I have no doubt she's very much alive."

When we got to my house, Matt parked the car and made the call. I could hear Kate's voice from my side of the truck.

"Allie tried to kill herself tonight," he said somberly. "She's at the hospital and so are two detectives named

Zabriskie and Henderson. You and Cheyenne need to get in your cars and go over there and tell them what happened on Saturday night." He paused. "Why?"

I couldn't believe she was being so stubborn about this—especially after what had happened to Allie.

"Because," he said, "that's what Erin wants. And she won't rest until you do. Enough is enough, Kate. This needs to end."

Kate said nothing. Then she hung up.

Matt tossed the phone on the seat. "I tried."

"If she doesn't go to the cops, then she has no soul. Speaking of which, is that who I think it is?"

I jutted my chin toward something black, camouflaged under the majestic oak by our driveway.

"It's a motorcycle," Matt said.

"It's not the bike. It's him," I said, pointing to the small orange glow ebbing in the shadows, indicating the lit end of a cigarette. "That's Stone Bone."

Matt gaped. "How can you tell?"

"Because he left a message in the guest book last night saying I had something he wanted."

"What's that?"

"A coffee cup he was using that I gave to the cops for fingerprints."

Matt shook his head. "You are such a badass."

I tried to stop grinning at him stupidly.

"Think I'll go introduce myself," Matt said, sliding out of the truck.

I watched as he coolly approached Stone Bone and coaxed him out of the shadows. Greetings were exchanged. They joked around and laughed. I sat there, totally confused. Were they friends? Had I been suckered into believing otherwise?

Matt lifted his right hand for a high five and Bone didn't leave him hanging. Fast as lightning, Matt delivered a neat uppercut with his other fist, smack into Alex's jaw so hard I heard the crack. Stone Bone went flying into his bike, which promptly fell over with a crash. He cursed and thrashed about.

Now I knew why left-handers didn't live as long as right-handers.

NINETEEN

Erin was laid to rest in Hillside Cemetery the next morning under the bright-blue skies of an Indian summer day. While the crowds at St. Anne's Catholic Church spilled out the door and down to the sidewalk, they respected the Donohue family's wish that the burial be private.

And so Boo and I, in our black suits, supervised from several feet away as Erin's coffin, draped with white lilies and roses, was carried from the hearse on the shoulders of several pallbearers, one of whom was Matt.

Standing at erect attention by their parked cruisers on the cemetery access road, Perfect Bob and Detectives Zabriskie and Henderson also observed. Waiting,

I supposed, for the moment when the coffin was lowered into the ground, the final good-byes were said,
and handfuls of dirt thrown.

Only then could they arrest Matt for the murder of
his former girlfriend.

Boo gave me a nudge. "Have faith," she whispered.

"They're here because they want to make sure he
doesn't flee," I said. At the bottom of the hill sat two
other cruisers, their blue lights flashing.

"It'll all work out," Boo said. "Trust your auntie."

The pallbearers placed the coffin on its brass winch,
and then Matt took his place next to Mrs. Donohue,
who hooked her arm in his as the priest asked God
to wipe from Erin her every last sin and reminded us
that, once dust, it is to dust we must return.

My mother activated the winch and the coffin lowered slowly while Erin's mother wept uncontrollably.
Matt bent down and took a handful of dirt that he gave
to Mrs. Donohue, who murmured a prayer and let it
fall. Everyone did the same until only Matt was left.
He bowed his head and said, "Peace," as he tossed the
final clump.

The priest closed his prayer book and everyone
bowed their heads.

"Into your hands, O Lord, we commit the body and
soul of Erin Anne Donohue." He made the sign of the

cross. "Peace be upon you who love Erin Anne and know that the Lord Christ himself promised that those who believe in him and with him will receive eternal life."

There were murmurs of "Amen" and then that was it. They lingered and hugged. Matt stood to the side as the Donohue family snaked their way to the limousines.

Bob went over to my mother while Detectives Zabriskie and Henderson crossed the cemetery. Matt glanced at me and winked, but made no attempt to run.

"I have to see what's happening," I said.

"Don't," Boo said. "Let him go."

It was too late. I ran as best as I could, despite my heels, which kept sinking into the grass. I could hear Mom say something like, "It's okay, Lily," but I didn't care. I needed to be there for him.

Detective Zabriskie turned to me, alarmed. "Is something wrong?"

I couldn't speak. It was the oddest of questions. "I guess that's what I should be asking you."

"Not as far as I'm concerned. It was a beautiful funeral." He gave my shoulder a paternalistic pat. "Sad, of course, but tasteful."

There were no handcuffs. No rights being read. And Zabriskie was acting like my long-lost uncle. "Aren't you going to arrest us?" I asked.

Matt laughed. "Thanks, Lil. What are you trying

to do, get me locked away?"

I was so confused.

"Oh," Zabriskie said, straightening. "I was sure you would have told her, but ... Well, last night at the hospital when we were wrapping up our questioning of Miss Woo, Detective Henderson and I were approached by two friends of yours, Kate Kline and Cheyenne Day, who wanted to amend their statements about what happened at Erin's house on Saturday night."

Matt raised his eyebrows. "Smart move, making the call to Kate."

"Apparently, both girls had been afraid that if they came forward and delivered testimony on one Alex Bone that said Mr. Bone would harm them." Zabriskie thumbed over his shoulder to Matt. "As luck would have it, however, your knight in shining armor here notified dispatch that he had just, uh, *taken out* Mr. Bone in front of the Graves Funeral Home and that he was worried Mr. Bone might follow through on various threats to do you harm as well, Lily."

I blushed.

Zabriskie continued. "Mr. Houser also managed to remember the license plate of the motorcycle, and we were able to apprehend Mr. Bone shortly thereafter and detain him on charges that he had violated his probation by driving under the influence and committing assault and criminal threatening. We are waiting to see if his DNA matches what we found under Erin's nails. In the meantime, he's not going anywhere."

Trying to get back into my good graces, Bob said, "See, Lily, the swab was worth it."

"Do you think he actually killed Erin, though?" Mom asked.

Zabriskie let Henderson answer that one. "What we know, according to the statements of the two girls who came forward last night, is that what appeared to have started out as Erin's infatuation with the older, more experienced so-called bad boy Alex Bone rapidly devolved into an unhealthy relationship. Mr. Bone imagined himself as Erin's liberator, introducing her to drugs, sex, and whatnot, while Erin became increasingly scared of his attempt to control her."

Matt said, "That explained her hot-and-cold attitude toward me. Wanted me to stay. Wanted me to go. I wished she'd just told the truth."

"So what happens next?" I asked.

"Next, we take Matt down to the station so he can write up a statement on his altercation with Mr. Bone and positively ID him," Henderson said. "Then we hope to do a lineup with the Krezkys to see if he was the man they saw arguing with Erin on Saturday night."

Not likely. Sara said the Krezkys told her that guy

was the spitting image of Matt.

"The fingerprints on the cup you gave us did match ones we found on a bottle of formalin in Erin's house," Bob said. "Excellent work."

Mom beamed. So did Bob.

"Alex was soaking cigarettes in formalin and selling them," I said.

Henderson nodded. "We executed a search warrant earlier this morning. Possession of neither formaldehyde nor tobacco is illegal, though." He sucked his teeth. "There's a legal loophole that needs to be closed."

That was it, then. The nightmare was over. Alex Bone had killed Erin, as I'd suspected, and Matt wasn't going to jail, and neither was I. Ten minutes ago, I'd been certain he was about to be arrested and now, not only was he free, but Zabriskie had called him a knight in shining armor.

"Can you give me a minute?" Matt asked, as Henderson and Zabriskie made to go back to their cruiser.

"One," Zabriskie said, smiling. "We're on a tight schedule."

Matt took me aside. Placing his hands on my shoulders and touching his forehead to mine, he said, "Okay, I'm leaving with these dudes to do the paperwork, but when I'm done I'm coming back and you and I are going to start all over."

I smiled. "What do you mean, all over?"

"No lies. No bullshit story about needing to pass an exam. No crazy girlfriend. Just the two of us. Alone. Finally." He put his lips to my ear. "We've got a lot of making . . . um, up to do."

A tingling danced across my heart. "Meet me in my garden at five?"

"Five it is. I can't wait."

Of course, I still had questions. For example, the Persephone necklace. How did that end up snagged on a tree in Erin's backyard the day after the murder? Then there was the issue of the man Erin was seen arguing with.

Alex Bone was thin and lanky, with long black hair. I supposed the ponytail might have accounted for it appearing short, but he bore absolutely no resemblance to Matt, whose broad shoulders and height alone distinguished him from Bone.

But since the police had cleared Matt, I was positive there had to be a reasonable explanation. It would emerge eventually, I was sure.

After cleaning up Erin's gravesite, I went home, took a long, hot shower, donned my short black dress, which I paired with fishnets, slipped my feet into a new pair of suede boots, and climbed through my window to the garden.

The stars were out, hardly visible above the dark, bare branches in the twilight, and they imbued the garden with a magical feel. Matt was leaning against the wall, waiting.

"Hey," he said, coming toward me.

"Hey yourself."

We stood inches apart. I let myself take in everything: the Panthers jacket, the whiteness of the clean button-down shirt underneath, how he smelled of shampoo and Irish Spring soap with a hint of jock.

He reached out and stroked my cheek. "We can go somewhere. Or . . ."

I didn't want to wait. I'd done enough of that. "Or what?"

"Or . . ." His hand slid behind my head, running my hair through his fingers as he bent down. Our lips touched briefly, and then again as I pulled him to me and his arms wrapped around my back.

He lifted his mouth from mine and kissed my ear, then my neck, sending electric shocks down my middle to my thighs, my toes, and everywhere in between. He pushed me against the garden wall and sucked my lower lip, and then kissed me deeper. I felt his hand on my waist, exploring.

"Hold on," I said, pushing him away. "I live in a house with three other woman, including my very perceptive grandmother on the top floor."

"Yeah?" he said, tracing the sinews of my neck with his lips.

"So, we should go somewhere else."

He planted a kiss on my collarbone. "Where?"

Anyplace but my house. "We could go to the tomb. No one will find us there."

Matt stopped kissing me and grinned. "You don't want anyone to find us, huh? You sure that's safe?"

"I don't care about safe." And I boosted myself over the wall.

Matt and I made it all the way to the cemetery and, having hidden the truck on a side alley in case Perfect Bob was on patrol and still trying to suck up to my mother by turning me in, we were about to sneak through the hole in the fence when my phone blared.

"It's Sara," I said, feeling a tug at my heart.

Matt groaned. "Don't answer it."

"I have to. She's leaving tomorrow straight after church and I won't talk to her for probably a year." I pressed Answer. "Hey!"

"Where are you?" Sara's voice was thick, like she'd been crying, and I knew, right then, that my plans with Matt were ruined.

"At the cemetery. Did you get my email?" I'd sent

her the rundown about Alex Bone and Kate and Cheyenne's last-minute crisis of conscience.

"Yeah, that's awesome. I'm so glad it's over and that Matt's not going to jail."

Matt put his head against the fence, frustrated.

"Are you stopping by to see me before I go?" Sara asked pitifully. "Tonight is our last chance. Mom's out buying stuff for the trip and Dad's picking up Brandon from a birthday party."

So it was as I'd suspected. It wasn't just Potsdam the McMartins decided had corrupted Sara. It was me.

I glanced at Matt. "Do you mind if we quickly run over to Sara's so I can say good-bye?"

"Do I have a choice?"

"Not really." I got back on. "Matt and I will be right over."

"Matt? Why not just you?"

"Because that's how it is, okay?"

There was a pause. "Okay."

I hung up and said, "Thanks."

"Doesn't matter." He took my hand and kissed it. "I'm in no hurry. We'll have plenty of time together after Sara leaves, right?"

For days and weeks to come, I would replay that line over and over.

TWENTY

What I remembered were the lights, bright and aimed directly at us.

We were on the long road out to Sara's development, which was so deserted, the city saw no need for streetlamps. I vaguely recalled flipping through my iPhone, looking for a certain song, and asking Matt a question, though I've since forgotten what.

I heard him swear. He jerked the truck to the right with such force that I was flung against the door, my seat belt cutting into my neck. The lights were incredibly bright. High beams? Everything happened in slow motion and my mind reeled with confusion. Stupidly, I wondered if he was swerving to avoid an animal or if, somehow, he'd drifted into the opposite lane.

It's odd, the random snippets that run through your mind when you are seconds away from death.

The truck more than bounced. It flew. Matt leaned on the horn as we seemed to surreally sail past the oncoming car, crossing the center line, into the ditch. Without his quick thinking, it would have T-boned us and I would have been a goner.

We rolled into a hedge and stopped, both of us shaking. The muscles in my arms and legs were taut with tension. I couldn't catch my breath.

Matt gripped the wheel and panted. "Are you okay? Oh, Jesus, Lil." He unclipped his seat belt and flipped on the overhead light, searching my face with such fear that I was frightened that maybe I'd been injured after all.

"I think so," I said, tentatively touching my cheek. "How about you?"

"Guess I'm fine, but . . ." He sat back, still breathing hard. "What happened?"

I checked the side mirror. The oncoming vehicle seemed to have landed off road, its red parking lights on. "Not quite sure, but whoever almost hit us is over there."

"God, I hope they're not hurt." Matt reached under the seat and retrieved an industrial-looking flashlight.

Then we got out and headed across the street.

The car had gone some distance in a field that, judging from the scent of fresh grass, had been recently hayed. My new suede boots were ruined as I trudged across the damp earth, keeping focused on the yellow circle cast by Matt's flashlight.

It illuminated the back end and the distinctive ridges of a Mercedes.

My heart clenched. I picked up my pace as we got closer, praying that it wouldn't be baby-blue, that it wouldn't be Sara's. But all hope was lost when the familiar numbers of her license plate were reflected in Matt's light. *TBX 25C.*

I let out a little yelp and ran to the driver's side window, which was down. A woman was slumped over in the front seat, blond hair tangled in a rat's nest.

The odor of alcohol was overpowering. "Oh my God!" I said with a gasp. "No!"

"You know her?" Matt asked.

It didn't seem possible. "It's Sara's mom, Carol."

Matt leaned in the window. "She's drunk."

"Do you see any blood?"

He flashed the light around. "Nope." He shook her shoulder. "Ma'am? Are you all right?"

Carol stirred and mumbled for us to go away.

Matt said, "That's not a good idea. How about we

drive you home?"

I pulled out my phone and dialed Sara, who answered on the first ring. "Where are you? Mom's almost home."

"Your mother nearly ran us over on County Road," I said, pausing. "I think she's been drinking."

Strangely, Sara didn't sound so surprised. "Is anyone hurt?"

Matt had managed to get Carol to a sitting position, though she was batting him away and telling him to let her be.

"I think we're okay, including your mother. Should I call an ambulance?"

"Geesh, no. Mom's on prescription meds, that's the problem. If the police find her . . . Look, can you just pile her into Matt's truck and I'll go back and get the car later? As it is, I'm without wheels."

The Mercedes was up to its front end in mud and what appeared to be leftover summer hay. This would be no easy fix. "We'll do our best."

"I'm sorry, Lil. I'll tell you when you get here what's been going on."

Adult issues, Mom had said. I felt kind of crummy for being so caught up in my own crisis that I hadn't paid attention to hers. "Hang tight. We'll be right there."

I hung up, and Matt handed me the flashlight. "I'll get the truck. You stay with her." He jogged off, leaving me to handle the mess that was Sara's mother.

Feeling super awkward, I knelt next to the open door, wishing this hadn't happened and also reminding myself how lucky it was that everyone was alive.

"It'll be all right, Mrs. McMartin," I said. "We're going to get you home."

Sara's mother swiveled toward me, her face bloated and red. "Is that you, Lily?"

I forced a smile.

Her chest started heaving and I panicked, thinking maybe she was having a heart attack or internal bleeding. "Are you okay?"

"It's my fault. I never should have gotten you into this." She was sobbing uncontrollably.

I patted her arm. "Do you think you can step out of the car? We'd like to get you home."

She threw one leg out, then another, leaning on me harder than I expected. When Matt returned with the truck, we managed to push and pull her into the front seat. I was sweating by the time we got her secured between us.

"This is mind-blowing," I said to Matt outside the truck while, inside, Mrs. McMartin slumped, jaw slack. "What do you think happened to her?"

"I think she's a drunk, Lil. Not much more complicated than that."

"But she doesn't drink. Her religion forbids it."

"Uh huh." He scoffed. "Wasn't she drunk at the wake?"

"Yep." I chewed my lower lip, trying to figure out what was happening in the McMartin family that would land Sara in lockdown and send her mother running for the bottle.

Matt slid into the driver's seat of the Mercedes and, after an appreciative assessment of its butter-leather interior, tried to start up the car. The wheels spun in the mud, splattering his truck. And me. "The damn rain and snow from earlier this week. The ground's too soft. I'm going to have to come back and push this out."

"I think we should get her home." Cars were slowing, curious.

"Agreed." He turned off the ignition, took the keys, and climbed behind the wheel.

Carol McMartin was passed out and snoring. Matt said, "Lovely."

"Never a dull moment," I said as we bounced out of the field onto County Road. "Not with Lily Graves."

Sara was on the doorstep, waiting with her arms folded, when we got to her house. She kept apologizing repeatedly as Matt and I held Carol between us and got her upstairs, Sara directing. Matt laid her on the bed and then left Sara and me to remove her shoes and tuck her under the covers, positioning her to the side in case she threw up.

"This is . . . so embarrassing," Sara whispered, closing the bedroom door behind her.

I thumbed to where Carol was passed out. "How long has this been going on?"

She shrugged. "A while, I guess. I'm not sure. All I know is that it's one of the reasons Dad's been so anxious to get us on a mission. He's convinced that if he sticks Mom in the outback of India, she won't be able to get her hands on any meds or booze." Sara grinned lopsidedly. "I suppose that's one advantage of being adopted, huh? Don't carry that alcoholism DNA."

I opened my arms, and she fell into them, hugging me tight. "I don't know what I'm going to do without you, Lil. You've seen me at my best and now my worst. You're the only one who knows all my secrets."

"Ditto." And then I had a brilliant idea. "Why don't you come live with me? We have plenty of room at our house, and that way you can finish up senior year."

"I can't. I wish I could." She gave me a squeeze. "Thanks, but Dad needs my help with Brandon."

Now I understood why it had been Sara's duty to get her little brother ready for school and make his lunch.

She'd been shouldering all this parental responsibility for years and I'd been too self-centered to notice. Talk about being a crappy friend.

"Hey!" Matt called from the foyer. "If we're gonna get your mom's car, Sara, we better do it now before someone sees it and calls the cops."

I headed downstairs, with Sara following. "Let me go," she said, unzipping a suitcase and removing a pair of rain boots. "It's my car, and the cops won't be suspicious if I tell them I avoided hitting a deer or whatever and ran off the road."

Matt and I exchanged glances. He would have much preferred me, but Sara did have a point.

"Just keep an eye on my mother, okay? Dad should be home any minute and then he can take care of her."

Matt abruptly stepped past Sara and boldly kissed me full on the mouth. "I'll be back soon. Don't start getting safe on me."

I smiled and kissed him back. "Not a chance."

Sara, eyes wide, quickly averted her gaze and went out into the night. The door closed with a slam and Matt's truck started up, rumbling down the driveway. I went back to the kitchen and sat on a stool.

The house had been stripped bare. The dozens of family photos had been removed from the white walls, along with Mrs. McMartin's watercolors of sunsets and her needlepointed SINCE GOD COULD NOT BE EVERY-WHERE, HE CREATED MOTHERS.

Everything was being dismantled, I thought. This house. This family. Sara and me. Our whole world.

There was an awful retching coming from the master bedroom. I ran upstairs and opened the door to a sickening odor of vomit. Mrs. McMartin was crying, her front covered in puke.

"Help," she pleaded.

Bringing my hand to my nose, I ran to the bathroom, grabbed a roll of toilet paper, and returned to find that she'd undressed down to her underwear, her clothes heaped on the bed. "We need to hide these before Sara's father finds out," she mumbled. "I need a shower."

She stumbled into the bathroom and closed the door with a slam. I flicked on a bedside table lamp and, seeing that the sheets had been ruined too, decided to wash them as well. The shower turned on. There was more vomiting.

I yanked back the comforter and the top sheet. The fitted sheet, however, was fastened to something at the footboard. Slipping my hand between the mattress and the box spring to unsnag it, I cried in pain as something sharp cut into my finger.

Blood streamed down bright red as I cursed

whatever had gotten me. A nail? Wrapping my finger in the sheet to stem the bleeding, I hoisted up the corner of the mattress and stared dumbly at what lay before my eyes.

Two silver scalpels and what appeared to be a man's shirt, speckled with dark-brown splotches of dried blood.

I shrieked and let the mattress fall. The shower turned off and Carol stuck her head out. "Oh, Lily, you don't need to do that. I'll change the sheets. You just go on and say good-bye to Sara."

Then she closed the door and turned on the water again. Did she know what was hidden at the foot of the bed? Did she know . . . *everything*?

I collapsed on the floor, reeling. Facts that had seemed so disjointed before now fell into place, creating a picture almost too gruesome to be true. Dr. Ken was a doctor. Erin had interned in his office the summer before. He was older and married, and naturally she didn't want anyone knowing they were having an affair.

Neither did he, especially after he learned she was pregnant. Allie had said the baby's father was pissed. How pissed?

I thought of the scalpels secreted away in the bed. *That* pissed.

Poor Sara.

For a second, I didn't know what to do. My first instinct was to leave everything, go outside, and wait for Matt and Sara. I could claim that I felt ill and had to go home. I could pretend I never saw what I saw.

But if I did that, then Erin's killer would be in India by Monday, never to return.

Think, my brain commanded. Use your logic.

I went to the balcony off the master bedroom and unlatched the double doors, stepping outside to escape the stench of that bedroom. Sara and I used to pretend this was Rapunzel's tower when we were little girls because the balcony overlooked a dramatic wooded slope that bottomed out at the railroad track.

The same railroad track that ran behind Erin's house, I realized. Of course, that was why the last car the Krezkys saw was Kate's, because Dr. Ken came and left on foot. He had only to travel maybe a quarter mile at most before reaching Erin's backyard.

Erin would have let him in her sliding door, too, because this was a man she trusted—possibly loved. Her parents were out of town. Mrs. McMartin was probably passed out, drunk, so Dr. Ken would have had no problem slipping away unnoticed.

That Saturday night, knowing she'd be alone for hours, he'd brought with him the tools of her destruction in case she didn't comply with his wish. An abortion? Out of the question for both of them, since Erin was super Catholic and certainly that conflicted with Dr. Ken's religion.

Then again, so did murder.

Mrs. Krezky gave a statement to police that she'd peeked inside the Donohue house and saw Erin arguing with a male. The only problem was, why would she have told Sara he looked like Matt when Dr. Ken was lankier, like Alex Bone, with a dark beard?

Unless Mrs. Krezky never said that to Sara.

Because Sara never asked.

Let me do the talking.

Oh God!

My entire body began to tremble. The Persephone necklace. I'd just assumed that I'd lost it at the quarry. But actually, now that I thought about it, I had worn it at Sara's house the night before when I was sleeping over. I must have accidentally left it there and she kept it, conveniently hanging it on a tree in Erin's backyard.

Sara knew. *Sara knew.* And worse, she set me up to take the fall. I'd told Sara that Matt was worried Erin would harm herself. Matt knew he'd told me, but he didn't know I'd told Sara. So it kind of looked to him, or anyone else, like I used that knowledge to stage Erin's suicide. Even the formalin might have been an attempt to further link me to Erin's murder.

All those true-crime shows she watched. They made her the perfect accomplice to cover her father's crime. Because after all, in the McMartin household, family rules.

School, church, family. Welcome to my prisons, she'd said bitterly to Alex at the café.

Alex, who was innocent. Sara, who was guilty.

I fell against the glass doors, fumbling in my pocket for my phone. I had to call Matt and warn him. But my pockets were empty, and I remembered with a sinking feeling that I'd left my phone in my bag on the floor of his truck.

Landline! I had only seconds left as I ran around the bedroom searching for a phone. What was wrong with these people? Where was their freaking phone?

"Oh!" Mrs. McMartin exclaimed. "You're still here."

Steam wafted from the bathroom, providing barely enough cover for me to grab the evidence and go. I bunched up the scalpels and shirt in the bottom sheet and shoved it under my arm.

"Sorry," I gushed. "Wanted to wash this before your husband came home."

"Leave it," she said with a dismissive wave of her hand. "My goodness. I feel so much better. Must have been some bad shellfish I had at lunch. Thank you, dear, for coming to my rescue."

"No biggie," I said, shrugging. "Well, I'll let you get dressed."

"Lily?" she called as I headed to the door.

My fingers closed around the handle. "Yes?"

"I said . . . leave it." Her tone was like steel.

I waited two beats. Then opened the door and ran.

She came after me, screaming at the top of her lungs while I took the stairs two at a time, my precious bundle clutched in my arms. If I could make it to the door I'd be safe.

Too late. Dr. Ken was already waiting, Brandon in a Superman cape by his side.

I gazed into his dark eyes, so warm and kind before, and saw only calculating cruelty.

"Brandon," he said crisply. "Why don't you go to the basement and watch some cartoons?"

Brandon dutifully did as he was told. Dr. Ken closed the door, locking it. He dropped his eyes to my bundle, and then to his wife. "You too," he said. "Go."

Mrs. McMartin nodded numbly, and footsteps padded up the stairs. The master bedroom door shut, and then we were alone.

He sighed. "This is exactly what I didn't want to happen." He plunked himself down on a bench and opened his coat so I could see the handgun under his tweed jacket. "Give me what you found."

I held it away from him.

"Really, Lily? You're in my home. You're unarmed. And no offense, but Sara's told me how everyone in school thinks your death obsession is weird. The stars are not aligned in your favor."

"Matt will be here soon."

"I don't think so."

I fought a flutter of hysteria. "What does *that* mean?"

"What could I do?" He shook his head forlornly. "He ran my daughter off the road, didn't he? He was going to kill her with his truck just like he murdered Erin."

"That's a lie! Your wife drove into us drunk. We saved her. If it hadn't been for Matt, we'd all be dead."

"Oh, I don't think so." He smiled. "You see, I'm Dr. Ken McMartin, the well-known, much-loved pediatrician. I am an established, upstanding member of the community, and you and Matt are punks who break into cemetery tombs and, for all I know, commit Satanic rituals."

My jaw dropped. Where was he getting this stuff?

"So what version of this story do you think the police will buy," he said, "yours or mine?"

The bundle of evidence felt almost radioactive in my clutches. "I think they'll trust us. Matt and me. Two against one."

"Correction. One against one." He frowned. "I'm so very sorry. But when I found out that Matt Houser had tried to kill my daughter, I did what any protective father would do." He shrugged apologetically. "I shot him. Dead."

Nooooo. The word rang through my brain. "You didn't. Sara wouldn't let you."

The garage door opened, and we paused to listen. Please be a truck, I prayed. But it was only the soft hum of the Mercedes.

"Let's ask her ourselves, shall we?" Dr. Ken said, standing as the door from the garage opened and Sara walked in looking like death.

She regarded her father with a sneer of disgust. "I hate you. There was no reason to shoot Matt. He never would have known."

"Sara," Dr. Ken said in a warning tone. "I understand that you're upset. . . ."

"Upset?" Sara yelled. "We could have just gotten the car and left. No one else would have been hurt."

"And let him come here to find Lily dead or, worse, holding the evidence?" he asked. "I think not."

At that, Sara spun on her heels, her eyes not

meeting mine but focusing instead on the bundle of sheets. "Give those to me, Lil. Just let me have them and maybe we can work this out."

I held the bundle tighter. "Are you crazy?" I shot back. "You killed Matt. You covered up Erin's murder. You . . ."—and for some reason, this was even harder to say—"you lied to me! You never were my best friend, or even a friend at all."

"I did not kill Matt. You have to believe me," she said pleadingly, as if her words could change things. "Now, please, just hand over the stuff, or else Dad and I will have to take it from you." She paused, her eyes wet. "One way or another."

For a moment, we locked gazes. Everything about her was so familiar that she seemed almost part of me. They say babies can't distinguish themselves from their mothers when they look in the mirror, and that's how I felt about her. "Why?" I whispered.

Sara's lower lip trembled. "I had no choice."

Dr. Ken was coming toward me, hand outstretched. "Just be a good girl, Lily, and do as you're told for once."

A surge of rage raced through my veins. Throwing the bundle on the floor, I bared my nails like Erin had in the cemetery and tackled Sara's father. I came at him so hard, he was flung into the glass front doors before

I kicked his knees so his legs slipped from under him and he fell to the slate floor, his head hitting with a crack. He reached for his gun, but Sara was faster.

She stood over both of us, the gun shaking in her right hand.

My knee rammed into his genitals, rendering him temporarily defenseless, then I did as Boo had demonstrated and pressed my thumbs into his carotid artery and jugular vein, easy to find after years of practicing on corpses. He gurgled and flailed before his eyes bugged out and he collapsed.

Sara pointed the gun in my direction. "I'll have to shoot you now. That's the only way out of this."

I got up, disgusted. "Yeah, right. As if you could."

For Matt's sake and for Erin's, I summoned what little courage I had left and wrenched the weapon from her hand. Then I opened the door to toss it out, almost pitching it at Perfect Bob, who was there on the front step. With Mom.

No words were said as police officers swarmed the foyer, cuffing Sara and Dr. Ken. It wasn't until Mom took me into her arms that I broke down like a baby.

All I could say was, "Matt."

Later, they would tell me that all he could say was, "Lily."

EPILOGUE

The nondescript silver sedan that had been stalking Sara and me belonged to the undercover division of the Potsdam Police Department, on loan to Mom, who'd managed to convince her boyfriend that she needed it to tail her daughter. Which, looking back, explained why our tagger sucked.

My mother had been lagging behind when Matt and I stole away from the garden to go make out. So she hadn't been there to witness Carol driving into us drunk--an accident that definitely hadn't been part of Dr. Ken's plan. If Carol hadn't made that mistake, there was a good chance the McMartins would be living in India, free from prosecution.

Then again, as Boo would say, there are no such things as accidents or coincidences.

It was Boo who'd spied Matt and me sneaking out, and by the time she'd tracked down Mom, I was already at the McMartins' putting Carol to bed. Fortunately, I'd left my iPhone in Matt's truck and, unbeknownst to me, that's how Mom had been monitoring my whereabouts—by plotting every movement of my iPhone on her Mac.

That would have pissed me off royally. Before.

But I was surprisingly cool with her overprotectiveness when I learned that because of it, Mom found Matt before he lost too much blood and managed to stem the bleeding, using her awesome anatomy knowledge, while simultaneously calling in the entire Potsdam PD to come to my rescue.

Matt was rushed by ambulance to the hospital, coherent enough to tell them that I was at Sara's before he passed out completely. By the way, it was Sara who called Detective Henderson from the Potsdam Regional Medical Center to say that I'd been at the cemetery with Matt. He'd remarked that she wasn't a friend. He'd been so right.

What will happen to Sara and her father is for the courts to decide, and I'll leave it at that. They say justice comes from the law, but forgiveness comes from the heart. Matt says I need to forgive Sara for me, not for her. I don't know. Maybe one day I'll be able to.

These days, Matt and I are just concentrating on getting back to normal. Funny, I used to despise that word, and yet I cannot imagine any state sweeter than the one I'm currently in—madly in love.

Finally, for Matt and me, that's no secret.

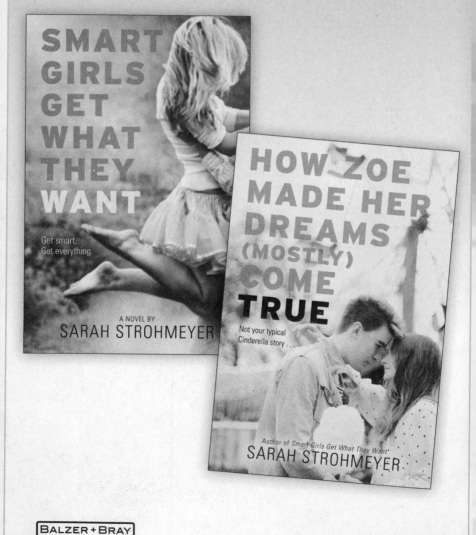